UPTOWN BLUES

SETH PEVEY

For Eileen, with love and gratitude.

ONE

When Louis Armstrong was a small boy, his father left him.

None of the books I read say much about why he left or where he went, just that one day Papa Armstrong was gone. That's the important bit of the story.

Louis was probably too young to say goodbye, or to even understand goodbyes as huge as that one, which would have been one of those life-changing ones that you have to try and remember forever. Except, you never really know which goodbyes *are* such a kind, do you?

I think about little Louis a lot, can almost see him sometimes. I can see his mama just set him down at the supper table one evening, can see her sadly ringing that porch bell, not really expecting an answer from down the alley. But she still rings it anyway, stares down to the empty end of things. When no one comes, this now smaller Armstrong family sits and eats but leaves Daddy's seat at the table empty, and nobody touches his chair or his plate. I can see them, even if the books don't have much more than a sentence or two about the whole thing.

I think that *my* daddy would never ever do that. Not on purpose. He'd never leave me if he had a choice. At least, he wouldn't leave forever. He's not around all the time, but that's because he's a *hard-working man*. From four to midnight, every day, Daddy is gone. He makes the streetcar go, gladly rings the bell (clang clang clang) all of the evening hours. You can hear him, and it doesn't matter where you happen to be in the smile, which is what I call Uptown because the river curves in a big smile shape and so do all the streets. Daddy's route even looks like a smile, too, because it matches the path of the river. Up and down and up and down Carrollton Avenue he goes smiling, and then over by us in the Seventeenth Ward, where he turns the seats all around and goes back again. But my daddy always puts the streetcar back in the big shed and comes to supper just past midnight. He even eats the same meal just about every night. I'm in bed when he comes, but I listen for his boots to land happily on the porch (thunk thunk) and his chair to be tiredly pulled back and his waffles to go launching up from the toaster. Daddy is *the only man in the world who likes to dip waffles into red beans*, Mama Jones says. I tried it once but only once. Like Louis, I prefer cornbread all the way.

I do get to see my daddy every day, though. Mr. Julian's studio is too far away from the Seventeenth. So is Mrs. Weinberger's clinic. Last but not least, my favorite—Mr. de Valencia's fancy home is also too far away. None of them live near the Seventeenth, but they do all live in the smile, right about where the nose would go, which is around where Napoleon crosses St. Charles. And so, every day when I finish my appointments, I get to walk out into the neutral ground with my horn and wait for Daddy to come on by in his streetcar and *scoop me*.

But today.

Today was a bad day. There were dark clouds in the sky and Mrs. Weinberger had asked me beaucoup questions and Mr. de Valencia had run out of petit fours. I had a dark feeling about things, standing there in the neutral ground with my horn and my backpack and knowing that it was just about to rain on me. Cold, too.

All of the streetcar drivers know me, of course. They all wave or tip their hats and Mrs. Washington even throws me a chocolate on most days as she rolls on by. But not today. She went on in a hurry. I think maybe when the rain is coming, people treat the conductors more rudely. I could see folks in her car who were looking mean out at all the big houses and magnolias. The streetcars are stacked, so I knew the next one, which was going to be Daddy, was coming along directly.

I know perfectly what the clang clang on Daddy's streetcar sounds like, because it is just a little happier than the others and that makes it different. I think this is because there's a chip on the old bell about the size of a chiclet missing, and it makes the notes hop just that little bit higher. You take something out, you get something new. It's the same way small horns sing higher than fat ones; the same way people do.

Every day, when I hear it, I smile. And that was what happened today. *Clang clang*, and I knew Daddy was coming, just a pinpoint under the oaks but getting bigger every second.

When he finally got to my stop, Daddy hoisted open the old streetcar door for me and gave me a big smile because he is not someone who catches dark feelings, even on rainy days when people are rude and don't have correct change, or are short altogether, which is what happened next.

A tall lanky fellow wearing dirty cooking pants and a tight white shirt cut right in front of me as I was trying to board. He smelled like smoke and nasty beer, so I tried to keep my distance. He messed around with the stuff in his pockets for a minute, mumbling something under his breath, before he turned to face me.

"Hey, kid, you got a quarter?" he said, in a voice that made me think he might shake it out of me if I said no.

I stared at him.

"Kid?" he said again, his eyes flicking down to the horn I had in my hands, which made me grip it very tightly.

Daddy chimed in just then, tapping the passenger on his shoulder, taking the dollar and then nodding to the back of the streetcar as if to say, "Don't worry about it."

Then Daddy pulled the missing quarter out of his own pocket, winked at me, and slipped it into the machine.

People say that my daddy is one of the most handsome men in the Seventeenth. But one of his front teeth is chipped just like the bell on his streetcar, and his smile, even though it is one of the biggest you've ever seen, always seems a little crooked—like if Tchoupitoulas Street had to make a detour around construction. But his uniform is always clean and starchy and his boots are always polished because *a man takes pride.* He smiled at me and I smiled back.

Then I swiped my special RTA card, which has

Daddy's name and face right on it. It lets me ride any bus or car in the city for free, anytime I want.

"Where you at, junior?" he said, which is what he always says. I didn't say anything, which is what I usually say. But now I hate myself for that, and I wonder what Louis Armstrong would have said if he knew that his goodbye was the kind that it really turned out to be.

I have a special favorite chair on Daddy's streetcar, which is, of course, the conductor's chair. It's on every car, actually. The thing about a streetcar is that it has two conductor's chairs. It has the one that's in the front, where the conductor sits, and then the one that is going to be in the front in the future, just as soon as the streetcar gets headed in the other direction.

Daddy always says if there is another person sitting in the backwards conductor's chair, *you're not allowed to get upset, because that's every kid's favorite chair and you ain't royalty.* But telling someone they are not allowed to be upset is a pretty silly thing to do because you either are upset or you aren't. What's for sure is that I'm not allowed to stand and stare at the person until they move, which is something I used to do all of the time before Daddy's boss fussed at him about it. *Someone must have complained,* he said, and didn't smile at me for a whole hour, which felt like that part of "Saints" where it goes on about how *the sun refused to shine.*

There are a lot of things like that. Things I don't know how to do quite right. That's why I go to see Mr. de Valencia. He is a fancy man in a big fancy house and he *knows how to make people feel comfortable with his behavior.* That's what Daddy said about him, and he was right. When I see him and he speaks gently to me with his accent all funny, I do feel beaucoup comfort, and I understand why they call a person like that a "gentle" man. I like Mr. de Valencia. He is the only one who seems to know and to understand why I don't speak much. The others (Mr. Julian and Mrs. Weinberger especially) can't seem to wait for me to open my mouth. I don't know why. But not Mr. Valencia. He pours me tea and gives me petit fours and talks to me about things. He says you should always hold open doors, walk with good posture, don't slurp soup or burp at the dinner table. Sometimes he talks about things which I can't understand and other times I blow my horn for him. He is an old man in a wheelchair and when he smiles, which doesn't happen too much, I can tell he means it. I like Mr. de Valencia.

Anyway, today there was no one sitting in the backwards conductor's chair. In fact, there were only three other people on the whole entire streetcar, including the lanky man without proper fare. It has been *mighty slow lately,* as Daddy had been saying quietly to Mama Jones over his waffles, maybe thinking I couldn't hear. Daddy worries about slow because of *downsizing and layoffs*. But I love it, because I get to sit in my favorite chair. I kind of feel like Daddy when I sit there, and sometimes I even like to pretend that that is exactly who I am.

But today I was thinking of something else. I looked out at St. Charles Avenue moving away from me, like the whole world was in reverse, which it was. Oak branches were there for just a second and then they were gone on down the road. People would go from frightening-big to small and their voices from forte to piano. Cars pulled into the neutral ground and made big turns as soon as we passed by, and bikers crossed the tracks. But it was like everything I saw had already happened. It was different from riding up front and seeing everything waiting to happen. I was thinking about the way things can happen only once. They happen big and then they get smaller and smaller until you can barely see them until the *vanishing point* eats them right up.

I remember I was thinking that because that is when *it* happened.

Where Mama Jones and Daddy and I live is called a shotgun. It is painted a color which I think is purple but Daddy calls *grape* when he gives instructions to the pizza man or the Chinese takeout man. I happen to know that a real shotgun is black and gray and wood-colored and not even close to grape. I don't like how our house is called a shotgun. That's because I know the sound a gun angrily makes.

Poor little Louis Armstrong. He is sitting at the supper table and Daddy's chair is empty. His life is missing love from the very get-go. He doesn't know yet that one day it will fill back up, that it will flood, that it will go over every levee and every bank. He doesn't know yet that he will drown in love one day. All he knows is that Daddy is gone. Right in that moment, he can't even see the thing getting smaller and smaller and moving away from him. All he knows is that he has to grow up now without love beneath him.

Pop. Clang. Scream. Shatter. Moan. Scream. Crash. That's the sound a gun makes.

My knuckles go white against my horn. I grip it so tight I can feel the muscles inside my fingers start to unwind, to burn. The streetcar keeps going. It runs right through the light on Oak Street and into a big blocky SUV, which it crumples like a paper cup and pushes for another few feet before finally coming to a grindy stop. I am thrown to the ground, and by the time I get back up on my feet, the other three people who were on the streetcar have already left. I can see the backs of them running down Oak Street, away from us. I can see the fear in the way they move, and I know it is terrible because I feel it now too. But I don't run, not at first. My heart is beating from deep inside my head, making me dizzy, making it hard to see or move or think.

Daddy is still in the front conductor's chair. He doesn't move. I wonder, for a moment, why he went and let the streetcar crash like that, even in an emergency. Daddy is one of the best drivers in the RTA and has a *perfect record*. I try to take a step towards him, but my legs have gone cold and stiff.

I manage to step one foot after the other, pushing myself forward down the aisle using the backs of seats, until I make it to Daddy. He still has his hand on the lever that makes the car go.

I want to call out to him, but I am scared. I put my horn to my lips and just stand there, not making a sound. I stare at Daddy for a long minute, but he doesn't make a move. I can hear something drip dropping out of him onto the metal floor and going plunk, plunk, plunk.

I can't see Daddy's face. I mean, I can look at it, but I can't see it. There is just a blur there. Not even a blur, but more like a completely invisible thing, like the black box when they show titty on television. I try to rub my eyes but I still can't see it. Something in my brain, all hazy and blurry, has gone haywire and just won't see.

By now, a gray-headed man has pulled open the door to the streetcar and is standing over Daddy, saying, "Jesus Christ, Jesus Christ. Call an ambulance, Gina! Call an ambulance!"

Daddy still doesn't move.

I give Daddy a big hug, my horn still in one hand so that it bangs on the dashboard of the streetcar. The man yelling about Jesus is pulling me away, but I don't want to let go. Hands are yanking me free, prying me, tugging me away. I can't fight them, because there are too many, and the next thing I know I'm standing out in the neutral ground facing a circle of people who all want to ask me questions.

"What happened?"

"Do you know this man?"

"Did you see what happened?"

"Are you okay, kid?"

I don't like questions. And I especially don't like it when people ask them at me, even when I'm feeling happy and good and safe, which is not even close to how I feel standing there beside the smoking streetcar all banged up and poking into that SUV, with a daddy that hadn't moved or taken a breath when I put my arms around him, and I think—

I think about Louis Armstrong. He's a tiny child and sitting on his porch. He's looking down his downtown street in the evening, looking through the gas lanterns and past the stray cats and waiting to see if Daddy will come home again. All of the things that Louis will be in his life are waiting to happen. He will become famous. He will play Carnegie Hall. The airport in New Orleans will be called Louis Armstrong International. He'll be on a postage stamp and his music will be sent out into space for aliens to find. But for now, he is just a lonely boy in a bad neighborhood with a horn and Daddy is gone and rushing away to the *vanishing point* at the end of the street that has already swallowed him up forever.

I run. The Jesus Christ man goes to grab me, but I dodge out of the way and I'm gone. I've always been a fast runner. There is none of them, especially not Gray Hair, who is going to come close to catching me. My backpack is bouncing on my back and I'm swinging my horn out in front of me until my legs have come fully back to life. Then I'm flying.

Down Oak Street I run off into the neighborhood until I can't hardly breathe. My heart is crazily thumping like a scat singer. For a while, I hide in Mrs. Lafreniere's carport. I hold tight to my horn. I wrap my hands around the cold brass and I rock for a while, press it to my lips but don't blow. The brass doesn't shine bright. It is red now, slippery. My shirt is also red. The sun is also red, hanging low in the sky, and I know it will leave the smiley face soon and I sit there wishing it would take me with it.

Mrs. Lafreniere comes out, and when she sees me she screams. I know she likes discipline and church and I'd never heard that kind of sound come out of her.

But her scream is real short and high—just a yelp. She puts her hand to her chest and takes a deep breath, during which her shoulders sag a bit and I have the sense that she is mad at me.

"What on Earth happened to you, child?"

Her eyes are getting wider the longer she looks at me. I start to cry.

She grabs me by the wrist and goes to gently twisting me this way and that. She lifts my shirt and runs her old hands against my chest with a worried look in her eyes. The wrinkle lines have gotten so deep on her forehead that they look like the bars on a sheet of music.

"This ain't your blood, Andre. Whose blood is this? Look at me, child. Andre, whose blood is this?"

I start to pull away, but her grip is strong and I can see that she is not scared but that nothing else in the world matters to her right then.

"Come on, baby," she says and opens the door to her noisy Pontiac.

It is dark by the time she opens the car door again and tugs me out onto the street in front of our grape shotgun. In our driveway there are three police cars with their blue lights flashing, and strange men in uniforms are standing out front and watching me.

Then I hear Mama Jones screaming. It's a good three octaves above the sound she makes when she stubs her toe. It's more pitiful than the wailing she does when one of her stories ends with the lovers all heart-broken. It's got more terror in it. The scream is bouncing all down the street and has people coming out onto their porches and looking down at us. When I hear that scream I know that it is something I will always remember, no matter how much time were to pass.

One of the officers has an arm around Mama Jones, but I can tell he doesn't really mean it. It is more like the kind of arm you'd put on an animal that was misbehaving. An arm for control, not for comfort. But Mama Jones isn't paying any attention to him anyway. She is staring up at the sky and not paying attention to me either while she shrieks and moans.

One of the officers steps towards me, and Mrs. Lafreniere gives me a little gentle push forward. Then she slowly backs up to her Pontiac and gets in and shuts the door with a loud thud. I can see her watching for a second out of the corner of her eye, but then she drives away, her sagging tailpipe skipping and bopping over the potholes.

The officer is still moving towards me, faster now. He has a big gut hanging over his tool belt and his face is not gentle. The opposite of a gentleman. He has not shaved and I can smell some kind of cigar coming off of him. There is a gun on his belt, big and black and heavy. I don't trust a thing about him and I'm holding on tight to my red horn and feel myself start to step backwards. I don't want this man to touch me, don't want to hear his voice, don't want to hear Mama Jones scream or see the porch people all looking over long-necked like the egrets in the park.

All I want is to hear Daddy's boots on the porch, his chair scraping back, his waffles popping. *A man takes pride,* I want to hear him tell me.

The officer takes another step towards me, and I see his hand go to his gun just for a second and then fall by his side. I know he didn't mean it. I know that he is touching his gun in the same way that I'm gripping on to my horn, but I don't care. I don't want anything to do with this—with these officers and their bright lights and hard looks. I don't want them taking me somewhere with more guns and more lights and more strange fat men with stubble on their cheeks. I open my mouth to tell the officer as much, but no sound comes out.

He gets a hand on me and I start to go dizzy. Everything is blue flashing lights and Mama Jones screaming. There's a feeling in my head like when you turn to a dead channel in a hotel room and the screen roars black and white and fuzzy at you. All I know is that I'm being pulled away, to a place where I don't want to go. Then I feel a tug at my horn—someone is trying to take it from me, which is something that no one should ever try to do. I swing out with my free hand, and before I can even think about it I feel the officer's big gut try to swallow my fist. He calls out in an angry voice, but I'm already running away down the dark street with my horn held out in front of me and my backpack bouncing. The blue fades away and now there are only yellow streetlights and I'm running down as far as I can see, hoping I'll vanish somehow and this will all be over.

But of course, that's not how it turns out at all.

TWO

Tomás de Valencia had lost a great many things in the course of his life. So many, in fact, that he had become a great master in the art of loss.

First were his brother and his country. Next went the ability to father children—a kick from a devilish horse had seen to that. He'd been so young, but he'd continued to live past it and accepted two boys of another blood and raised them as his own sons.

Then he'd lost one of those boys, too. *Insult to injury*, as they said. Robert Herbert had been such a joy.

Soon afterwards, he had lost his best friend in the world: the father of those boys. How long had it been now since that day in Audubon Park, when Marcus Herbert had collapsed into the black bayou with his second and final clot in the brain?

And now the latest loss—his ability to walk.

Months of pain and attempted rehabilitation had left him chairbound, likely for the rest of his days. And still he lived on. Still he persevered. Past it all, he emerged a great statesman of deprivation, a sage of absence and forfeiture.

Tomás de Valencia rocked his wheelchair gently and thanked God for all of the joys that were still his. It was a sort of prayer he practiced every night, listing all of the things he had managed to hold on to after so many battles. He counted these blessings with a ritual regularity and discipline.

First, he still had his cast-iron dignity. There was also the warmth of golden sunshine on his face by day, a cool drink of an evening, the lady of the house to fuss with. She was out of town now on some far-flung plea-sure cruise, leaving him to the flavor of his thick cigars. These were a pleasure he only allowed himself in her absence, as the smell of them would arouse her allergies.

He also had the exploits of his still-living "son" Felix Herbert to follow, and those intrepid tales came as fast and as engaging as an old man could hope to keep up with. A private detective's life was full of adventure and bravado, after all, and Tomás had pride to spare for the boy, now turned into a fine man.

And last, but perhaps not entirely last...

Well, he simply didn't like to dwell on it. But it could not simply be overlooked when counting God's many graces. The simple truth was this: an immense fortune didn't hurt either. It was worth thanking the universe for, once in a while. Tomás de Valencia was not a man for worldly things, but what better way to lift your crippled spirits than a personal elevator installed at home? Nurses to help you anytime you required? The finest bourbon money could buy and leisure time in which to sip it while overlooking the springtime avenue?

And that was really the thing, wasn't it?

Time.

Tomás found himself, for the first instance in his long life, with *time* to spare. That, more than any other thing at this moment, was something he was immensely thankful for.

He filled that time with gusto and kindness, relishing it in the way only a man free from the salvos of bitterness could. Because there was one loss he would never abide, and that was the loss of his usefulness.

He'd tried a few different avocations out without finding any particular meaning: painting, violin, teaching Spanish. But a prime opportunity had arisen, just a few months earlier, to give private tutoring to so-called "at-risk youths" in the art of class, etiquette, and manners. And, if he threw in a bit of ethics and philosophy for lagniappe, who would ever make a fuss? Tomás had jumped at the chance to once again do this holy work of boy-rearing, the work that had given him such fulfillment and purpose in the past.

Well, he had rolled at the chance anyway. His jumping days had gone.

It was a cool evening now, the air along St. Charles Avenue going crisp and petal-smelling. The parades had passed weeks earlier and the austere season of Lent lay heavy on the city. Tomás watched the streetcars rattle by and appreciated the horse-clopping regularity of the Roman Candy carriage as it retreated for the night. But not all was meek and regular, and there was one blight on the peace of the Avenue—scores of NOPD cruisers blustering their way upriver with sirens and lights blaring, a new cluster of them coming through every ten minutes or so, each pack with its own doubled-down sense of urgency. So many, he thought, that it must portend something awful. That set Tomás to envisioning all of the awful things that went on in the world beyond these stone walls, and so he retreated to the back balcony, lest his bourbon be spoiled by a foul mood.

Though it certainly lacked the life and activity of the Avenue, from his backwards-facing perch, Tomás could overlook one of the best-kept half acres in the entire city, with Bermuda grass meticulously clipped, fountains of pure white marble, Romanesque columns and a pantheon of statues. All of it was centered around an inviting gazebo, with a grand live oak sprawling over all as it had for centuries.

He was hoping to hear the whip-poor-will that had taken up residence in that majestic oak. So much better than sirens to accompany an old man's peaceful thoughts. It was usually at this hour that the creature would practice its lonesome cry. But tonight, Tomás did not hear the bird. In fact, he heard no birds or squirrels or any wildlife coming from the backyard.

He sipped his drink, cleared his throat, and waited.

Such eerie silence. A slight breeze passing through the limbs of the oak, the distant wail of the sirens—that was all. Tomás peered out into the darkness. The lady of the house being away, Tomás often neglected to turn on the back lighting, preferring the light of the moon, which had by now grown fairly full and bright.

And so, squinting from his high spot, Tomás was able to catch a flash of something moving through the hedges.

Something larger than any squirrel.

The dark shape emerged and stood still on the perfect grass, its outline barely illuminated by the lunar glow. It stopped just between the replica of Michelangelo's David and the rustic rope swing hanging from the oak tree bough. The specter seemed to consider them both before finally placing itself in that swing and kicking out its lower appendages until the swing itself had been set in motion.

Tomás de Valencia's mind quickly ran through the catalog of what mortal enemies he had stacked up in his long and rambunctious life. He found quite a few, though all of them had been long ago bested. So, was this to be some random thief stalking through the Uptown district? If so, how had he found the time for a swinging session amidst his urgent art? Tomás began to think of the pearl-handled pistol, and of exactly what state it would be currently tucked away in his dead best friend's mahogany desk. He pictured himself trying to wheel there in a frenzy, only to return and find the shadow had disappeared into the night once again, or perhaps—

Just then, Tomás caught the glint of something metal in the apparition's hand. Whatever it was, this object reflected the moon's color quite clearly, flashing against the darkness with a dull shimmer. A long gun, perhaps? A weapon of murder? The old man, from his fairly helpless station, worried his gray beard with nervous fingers as he squinted down at this mystery. Could it be the barrel of a rifle? A stolen crystal pilfered from Madame's personal collection? Some other—

His guessing game was swiftly interrupted by a sound. Tomás de Valencia's mind struggled to understand what it was hearing.

He'd come to his backyard to listen for the whip-poor-will, but this was no bird.

And while it was a human sound—unmistakable, blue, old—it was as native and as familiar to that riparian patch of earth as the whip-poor-will itself. It too had a pure voice, a brilliant endurance of wind, and a tone so familiar that Tomás de Valencia could now recognize it just as easily as he could differentiate the distinct peculiarities of birdsong.

It was the sound of a trumpet blowing.

It was the boy. The boy who loved to sit on that swing and play echoing tunes under the cocoon of that live oak, Tuesday and Thursdays, just after his etiquette lessons were complete at three o'clock.

"Andre?" Tomás de Valencia's called out into the night, resisting an impotent urge to stand.

THREE

Retired police detective David Melancon's hair had finally finished going gray. It had been threatening to do so for thirty years and had finally backed up its bluff. There was only a pallid shock of it left now as well, and not a trace remaining of that once-dashing mane of blond. A trio of profound worry lines had struck across his expanding forehead, deepening as his misgivings did the same. He had arthritis in his knees, a back that hurt most every morning. The latter was probably his own fault. He now often slept reclining in a chair at his desk at the Basin Street Detective Agency, an expired *Picayune* draped over him and a ratty fedora pulled down over his eyes. His doctor had just recommended he start wearing some glasses. He'd had 20/20 his whole life, been a crack shot and a fine driver. Now that acuity, like all the other sharp weapons in his material arsenal, was becoming blunted by the passage of time. It was all like some twisted joke, getting old. Each part of him seemed engaged in an escalating entropy, all except for one.

His mind, at least in its own estimation, was as keen and as sharp as ever—a surprise, really, for a man who had spent so many years looking up at the world from the bottom of a bottle. Perhaps this was an unfortunate hand of cards to be holding, after all this time had passed. Sometimes he wished it was the other way around: that his mind would atrophy instead. He'd wake up one fine morning and find himself a simple, unworried creature, with the same blade of a body he had taken for granted at twenty-five. Turn the tables, let the intellect go to seed while his body aged like some sort of brilliant Italian libation. Oh, for that big, blond, flowing hair raining down his head in a devil-may-care mop, tanned muscles bulging under his jeans once again. While we're at it, a mustache that flamed Irish red at the tips. In this fantasy, all of it was his, yet he had not a care in the world because his brain had gone sour mash a long time ago. Fair enough trade. The things a man could do with a strong body and a mind too dumb to care. Such, anyway, were the imaginings of David Melancon's late nights, his meditations in this lemon of a body.

But that was not the way of it, and since he'd quit drinking a few years earlier, he'd had to find various ways of keeping that incessant head of his occupied. It was almost a matter of life and death, and silly fantasies only took you so far.

He reclined, almost lay back, in his office chair at the agency. He could never bring himself to crawl back to his dingy apartment in St. Roch these days. It was too quiet there. No wife, no children, not even so much as a dog to welcome him back.

And so, he stayed here, where his mind could at least pretend its constant rhythms had some music to them, a masquerade of enterprise, that it wasn't just a hollow dishwasher on an endless rinse cycle, long ago emptied of the night's Tupperware, spraying its essence right down the drain for naught.

He had a bag of Zapp's laid on his chest and was listening to his police scanner, reliving to himself his dashing days as a NOPD detective, before that organization had gotten the better of him. Though, if you had asked him why he insisted on listening to this late-night staticky drama, he would have lied and said he was looking for job opportunities, hot case leads and the like. Not that anyone did care enough to ask him.

It was turning out to be a quiet night so far. *However*, Melancon thought to himself grimly, all you really had to do was wait around long enough and the bodies would begin to drop. It was the way of the city, the bestial nature of the place that would never lie dormant for long. It would have its bodies by sunup, its blood. There was just nothing dry about the place. For now: a few noise complaints, a truck parked off St. Charles had been lit on fire. Nothing to write home about, not yet, and Melancon drifted in and out of sleep. He really needed to pick a new hobby, he decided, about the time he awoke with a long strand of drool near down to his chin. Try out some woodworking or maybe buy a guitar, and there were plenty of good fishing spots within—

"We've got a possible 30-S situation on the streetcar line. I need EMS rollin'... Carrollton and Oak Street. I got one hit in the head. Possible...*pfffft*."

"Come back, Unit 203, you're breaking up."

"I said I got a possible homicide, Uptown at Carrollton and Oak Street. I got one...*pfft*...male shot in the head...I got...*pffft*..."

"10-4...You got any...any scrip on a possible perp?"

"No. I got nothing. Vic appears to be an RTA worker. Streetcar driver."

The dispatcher went quiet for a long moment and the scanner was silent. Melancon almost gave it a slap. "Christ," he said to himself, leaning forward and raining Zapp's crumbs all down on the old cypress floor.

"I need crime scene tape, barricades. I need all St. Charles line streetcar traffic stopped."

"Is the...pfft...is the vic still breathing...203?"

"No, he's...*pfft*."

"Repeat, 203."

"He's...hit in the head. No way. Goner."

"10-4. We'll get the crime scene unit there ASAP. Anyone else hit?"

More static on the line. Melancon leaned over to turn the volume up a bit.

The dispatcher went back and forth with the patrolman on the scene, finally lapsing into a jumble of numerical codes that Melancon had long ago forgotten the meaning of. But it didn't take a code breaker to get the gist, and the gist of it was a horrid nightmare.

"City worker," he said to himself, fiddling with the papers on his desk and slapping a handkerchief across his face. Melancon envisioned some poor shmuck just trying to make ends meet, gunned down over a road rage incident or maybe over the fact that the streetcar drivers never had any change to return to you, or who knew what else. Melancon turned the volume down as the interference seemed to be worsening.

He thought about it. Poor shmucks. This town was full of them. Every night the city would dine on a few, wake up in the morning without so much as a bit of indigestion. When your number was up, your blood went down in between the cracks in the cobble, watered the old live oak roots that kept the sidewalks all broken.

Poor shmucks.

He dozed again, half-dreaming about bullets that had flown by his own head, their trajectories all handled by an angel that had spared him the fate of poor shmucks like the one on the scanner. He might have dozed an hour, maybe two. Sleeping in that reclining office chair definitely did his old back no favors, but he found it was less lonely somehow. Instead of being an old man curled up alone in an empty house, he saw himself instead as manning some lonely lighthouse above a sea of cruelty. Dozing, yes, but poised to respond should the need ever arise.

That need arose sometime around ten p.m., when the phone rang. The old grandfather clock they had inherited with the lease was chiming at the same time as his old flip phone began to vibrate.

Felix Herbert, his partner.

"What's up, Felix?" Melancon answered groggily. "Everything okay?"

"Um...yeah...maybe." Melancon could hear excited talking in the background, the echo of a big room. He waited.

"So, Tomás called me. I'm at the house on St. Charles. This kid that Tomás tutors, he's kind of a... well, I don't know exactly what's wrong with him, but he's...he doesn't talk, and..."

"Cut to the chase, Felix, I'm a man without much time left. And I'm not very good with kids."

"He's got blood on him."

Melancon stood up, but the head rush that hit him bade him sit back down again and fumble towards a cold cup of coffee still sitting on one corner of his desk. He spat it back out again. At least a week old, with just a hint of the fungal about it. Noisy cars passed by below on Basin Street, just outside of the French doors, and shook him where he sat.

"Blood?"

"Yeah...like a lot of blood."

"Did you call the cops?"

"We're just about to. I just wanted to run it by you first. The kid is...well, physically, he's completely okay, but, you know, something seems wrong with him. I was thinking the cops might ask a lot of questions about why he was here. They might even think, don't know, but...Tomás is having a fit. He's getting on in years, and I hate to think of him being dragged down to the station in his wheelchair and—"

"I'll be right there, Felix. Just make sure the boy is comfortable. You did check him for injuries, right?"

Twenty minutes later, Melancon's decaying El Camino was pulling up by the curb in front of one of the city's most picturesque Victorian homes. Every time he visited, the house had a way of making him feel a pang of regret for things he'd missed in life. Not that he would have known what to do with a property so outlandishly out of proportion anyway. He stood between the two gas lanterns flanking the front door, finding it impossible to keep his hat on his head, and rang the doorbell.

Felix Herbert answered, looking more beaten and tired than a twentysomething had any right to be. Melancon's young partner was long of limb, with green eyes and what was usually a self-assured, zesty bearing. But not this evening. His skin was unusually pallid, and those green eyes were urgent and fraught.

"I still expect Tomás to answer the door every time I come," Melancon said. "I keep forgetting, about the chair...about the train. Seems an odd thing to forget, I guess, seeing as how I was standing right there. I suppose the mind cuts out some of the bad stuff, the nasty bits, when it really wants to. Where's the kid?"

As he stepped inside, the old detective was reminded of the opulence of the place. He tried not to linger, tried not to give away his blue-collar, slack-jawed amazement that such places even existed. Just inside the parlor, he found Tomás sitting in his chair.

Next to him, on the couch, was a little boy of maybe twelve or thirteen years old. The boy had a roundish face, partially covered by a curtain of thin dreadlocks. His brown eyes bored into Melancon with an intensity very far from childlike.

The boy had a blanket around his shoulders, was wearing an oversized Metallica tee shirt, and holding a cup of steaming liquid, to which he quickly averted his eyes once Melancon took a step closer. On the coffee table in front of him, a small trumpet had been set on a white handkerchief. Next to that, a silver platter of small finger snacks.

Melancon smiled at the boy, then walked over to the old man in his wheelchair and took his hand.

"Tomás." The two older men nodded at each other respectfully.

"Should we call the police, Detective?" Tomás asked. His eyes were heavy with bags and he wrung the wisps of hair on his chin.

"Probably," Melancon replied. "You don't have the parents' phone number?"

"I do have his home phone, but no one is answering. I left several messages on the machine."

"And how do you know the boy?"

"He was sent over by the junior cotillion. I've been tutoring him for a few months now. I'm not sure if Felix told you that I've begun teaching etiquette and manners to young people? Of course, the cotillion office is closed for the night."

Melancon nodded, shot a look at Felix, who was standing off to the side, his arms crossed and his bright green eyes regarding the boy.

The aged detective pulled at his belt and strode over to the couch. "Now what seems to be the trouble here, young man?" he asked, pinching up one of the cheese crackers from off the silver tray and using that casual moment to get a better look at both the trumpet and at the boy himself.

The young man, though tracing Melancon's movements with that same sober focus, did not respond. He sat still, and when he broke eye contact with the detective, he again looked down at his cup of cocoa and slightly flared his nostrils with a deep breath. Melancon took a closer study of him, more openly this time. The boy was clean, looked well-nourished. His head hadn't quite been grown into yet —a little large for the small, spare frame. But those intense wide eyes were so mature that they might have fit better in a grown man's face. Melancon scanned the boy's arms for scars, burns, marks of ill use, but he found none of the obvious signs of abuse or neglect, aside from a small scar on the boy's neck, old and faded enough to be irrelevant concerning the current state of affairs.

Trying another tack, the detective pointed at the bent, tubular brass sitting on the coffee table.

"Yours?"

But the boy was silent still, his eyes moving up to focus on the instrument where it softly gleamed in the lamplight.

"His trumpet," Tomás said, breaking the long silence that followed. "He's never without it. Carries it wherever he goes. It was how I found him this evening. I heard him down in the garden blowing it. When he stepped into the light, I was horrified to see the state of him. I kept his shirt in a freezer bag and gave him that old one to change into. I hope this was the right thing to do."

Tomás pulled a bag off the bookshelf behind him. A white shirt splotched with obvious blood, blackening now a bit with time.

"So, you came here because you were scared, I suppose. This man is someone you trust, I see. I see you are a good judge of character." Melancon smiled as he directed the line of questions at the boy, who again made no move to respond. Though this time he did sip his cocoa and stare at Tomás for another long, hypnotic spell before looking away again.

Tomás cleared his throat.

"Don't suppose you know his address?" Felix asked.

A sad shake of the head. "He resides in the Seventeenth Ward. Leonidas area, I believe."

"Rough part of town," Melancon said under his breath.

"Do you know your address, young man? Do you know your daddy's phone number?" Felix asked.

The boy winced. Clearly, unmistakably: a wince. A cringe, even. He looked down again, seemed to be biting at his lower lip. He picked the horn up from the table and cradled it in his lap.

"There was blood on that instrument as well," Tomás said. "I tried to take it from him to preserve the...evidence...but he was...unwilling to part with it.

I believe he must have washed it off in the bathroom."

Melancon grabbed a frilly ottoman, no doubt worth more than his car, and dragged it over to the edge of the couch. "What's your name?" he asked the boy.

More silence: complete and unassailable.

"Andre Adai," Tomás replied from his wheelchair.

"Can't seem to answer me himself, can he?"

Tomás cleared his throat again. "He does not speak, Detective."

Melancon blew out air, huffed a bit and ran his hand against his trouser leg.

"I can see that. The strong, quiet type. And from the Seventeenth? Yeah, I'm getting quite the picture."

The detective winked at the young man.

"Andre...I had a friend with that name growing up. I grew up in a pretty rough neighborhood myself. Lot of fighting and stuff. Is that what happened to you tonight, Andre? Did you get into a fight or something?"

The boy bit his bottom lip again. Just then, the old Westminster clock in the parlor chimed the hour. It had a lovely, light melodic tone that rang through the cavernous rooms of the mansion.

Andre looked towards it, and for the briefest of moments, a small slight smile played on his lips. Melancon watched as the boy bobbed his head, almost imperceptibly, along with the melody. The detective looked over his shoulder at the clock and then slid a little closer to the boy with his ottoman.

"You like that sound, Andre?"

The boy looked at the old detective again. By now the chimes had passed and he returned his pensive eyes to his mug, heavy sadness revisiting his features.

"He likes music," Tomás said.

"I see that. Now, Andre, I need to explain what is going to happen. Because we don't know how to get in touch with your parents, and because you had blood on you, we are going to have to bring you downtown to the police station. It's cold down there and uncomfortable, and they don't give you cheese crackers and cocoa. Now I'm not trying to scare you, but I'm just trying to explain to you like an adult that you can't just stay here. If you were in a fight or something, then that's okay, but you need to tell us about it."

But Andre was looking past him, over towards something in the corner of the room.

"Just can't get through to him," Melancon grumbled, biting his thumbnail.

"Ah, of course!" Tomás said from his chair. "I'd forgotten in all the ruckus."

He wheeled himself over to an old gramophone that sat in one corner of the room. It was angular, brassy, deliberately tarnished perhaps to give a patina of distinguished age. It was clearly an artifact meant more to be a conversation piece, an aesthetically pleasing reminder of days gone by, than an object of practical use.

"We have spent quite some time, Andre and I, listening to old records. Haven't we, my dear boy? You see, he adores jazz music. Sometimes, after listening to a few songs...well, that's the only time I've heard him speak at all. He might even say a small word or two. Although it was rare at first, it seemed to be getting more common as we became friends."

"That so?" Melancon asked, raising an eyebrow.

Andre stood up from the couch and walked over to a reading chair that was closer to the gramophone. He sat in it and nodded towards the record player.

"Ah, here," Tomás said, the delight clear in his voice. "Here is the very song he was playing when I found him in the garden."

As the needle went down into the old LP, Melancon recognized it right away: that ancient folk song about love and loss, a gambler's tune recorded forever in frozen oil by New Orleans' greatest son. The four of them all sat and listened to the sad dirge for a few minutes, listened to Louis Armstrong wail about finding his lover's remains stretched out on a long white table. Melancon noticed that the boy had begun to weep. No blubbering or shaking or moaning, just long tears rolling down from his eyes as he listened.

When the song was finished, the boy stared at the record player for a long moment, listening perhaps to the skipping it made as it spun out and delivered only a faint white noise. Then he went into his pocket and dug out a laminated ID badge. The young man stood up, handed the badge to Melancon, and went back and lay down on the couch with the trumpet held closely in his arms.

Melancon looked down at the badge: an RTA ID, short for Regional Transit Authority for the city of New Orleans. The man pictured was a middle-aged fellow with close-cropped hair, a chipped tooth, a round face and intense eyes—the spitting image of Andre.

"Renato Adai. Streetcar Operator," it read.

"Oh Lord," Melancon gasped, almost dropping the card and looking over at Tomás with a panicked expression on his face. The memory of what he had heard earlier that night on the police scanner came rushing back in an instant, the dots all connecting in the cruelest fashion.

Poor shmuck.

Poor shmuck's orphaned son.

Tomás's phone rang at that very moment.

FOUR

Louis Armstrong is thirteen and his daddy never did come back home.

He's the same age as I am now, has filled out a bit and grown taller, big enough finally for that face of his. But he is still a kid, a kid just like me. Louis lives a life that is filled with friends and enemies. He eats rotten vegetables out of garbage cans when the red beans run thin. He loves the sound of music that comes out of every door and alleyway in the neighborhood where he lives. He knows everyone in back of town.

Louis is on his knees staring down into a big cedar chest that one of his stepdaddies has left at his mama's house. There are some clothes, a bottle of whiskey, an old Bible, and a handgun big enough to blow a hole through a concrete wall.

And he is angry. But more than angry, scared.

They're kind of the same thing. Whenever someone acted nasty, Daddy always said, "Angry comes from scared."

Little Louis takes a swig of the whiskey, which burns him so bad he puckers and remembers his own boyhood. But then he scoops up the pistol, and his boyhood runs away again. He looks at himself in the mirror with it. He twirls it like he's seen them do at the Wild West show, but he's no good at it, nearly drops it on the floor. He's not a cowboy, and the pistol is terribly heavy and terribly dull, the shine having gone right off it. He rubs it with his shirtsleeve a few times, like a genie might come out, but it doesn't do any good.

It's New Year's Eve in New Orleans when Louis takes up that gun, and the night is dark and strange and loud with scary noise. The Great War in Europe is just about to start and will shrink all of those sounds and feelings, but right at that moment, it all feels like big magic when he heads out armed into the streets to see the blooming fireworks and dancing men.

The books get confused around this point. Some of them say that Louis was being bullied terribly by older, harder boys, and that that was why he scooped the gun. Others say it was just a happy thing, like bringing a string of firecrackers to a party. Some books say it was a way of defending himself from someone across the street with their own heavy pistol, and that he had no choice—kind of like why we have nuclear missiles, which is something Mr. de Valencia explained to me in one of his *ethical dilemmas*.

But I know *why*, know it much better than the books could ever say, because it's the way I feel right now. Exactly the way I feel.

Louis can't see the future, can't yet know how much love will come around later. He doesn't know he will climb the pyramids and play for kings and queens and show off, smiling, in Hollywood films that the whole world will smile back at. For now, all he knows is that he is young and alone, and so needs metal in his hands. He hasn't learned yet to tell one kind of metal from another. He hasn't learned the difference between brass and steel and iron and lead, because there has been no one to teach him.

I must have fallen asleep thinking about it—little Louis with that gun in his hand on New Year's.

I wake up and there is sunlight coming into a big room. I'm sweating and my heartbeat is uptempo, but there are soft sheets that smell flowery wrapped all around me. Nice sheets, silky-feeling against my skin. Something is not quite right. I don't smell red beans or hear music and I don't hear Mama Jones moving in the kitchen. For a second, I don't know where I really am. I grab for my horn, which is lying next to me on this big, ridiculous bed. For a second, I don't remember. But then I hear it. It is the clang, clang, clang of a streetcar passing by because I'm on St. Charles right in the nose of the smile and—

I'm hurting.

Suddenly I know I'll feel this way every time I hear the streetcar for the rest of my life, and that what used to be a happy sound has now changed forever. Hell, maybe I'm going to feel it every time I wake up no matter what I hear. I get out of the big bed and go stand out in the hallway in the PJs they gave me and listen real close for anyone moving around. No one seems to be awake yet. So, I'm walking around this big old house on St. Charles in borrowed PJs and I'm thinking about how it's going to feel to be hurting like this for the rest of my life.

It's not really even a house. It's a mansion. A museum. A collection of things that makes up a cold place where you almost can't believe some people live and shit and cook. It's almost not even real. I look at the things on the shelf. There's an elephant carved out of black wood. There are pictures in silver frames. There's what Mr. de Valencia calls the "Westminster clock," which I can hear chiming downstairs with its singsong jolly-old-England vibe. As soon as I think I'm to the end of the house, it just opens in some other direction and keeps on going. I look at all the books, all the records, all the bottles of wine. I push open one door and step inside a large office.

Here are more books than a person could ever read, and they're all a deep shade of brown. I look for a book on Louis Armstrong, but there don't seem to be any, which I find very strange. In the middle of the room is a large desk without much on it. Sunlight is streaming in from a big window and hitting right on the desk in only one spot, right where one of the drawers is. Is it a sign? I don't know, but I can't help myself from walking over and hovering my hand over the drawer handle.

I pull the drawer open and right there, sitting and looking up at me, is a pistol with a pearl handle. I know a little about a pistol because Daddy took me to shoot one a few times out on the West Bank. I also know that this is a revolver, and that all you have to do is pull that thing on the back, which is called a hammer, and then pull that thing on the bottom, which is called a trigger, and whoever it is who took something from you that can never be replaced will have something taken from them that cannot be replaced either.

I've never stolen a thing in my life because *a man takes pride*. Daddy always taught me not to do such things. But Daddy is—

Mr. de Valencia likes to talk about *ethical dilemmas* with me. Sometimes they involve different groups of people on different train tracks, which is awkward since I know Mr. de Valencia was hit by a train and that's why he is in his chair. But he doesn't seem to mind talking about train tracks. On one track is a school bus and on another stands you. You have the switch in your hands. Now, do you sacrifice yourself? Or do you save yourself and sacrifice the school bus full of kids? What if it's only two kids? What if it's only one? What if one of the kids will grow up and become Jack the Ripper? What if it's only one person, but that person is the one person in the world you need more than anything?

I put the pistol in the pocket of my PJs, hating myself, and run back to my bedroom. There I put it in my backpack.

For a second, I feel a train coming at me from somewhere. I think it to myself just like that.

Another ten minutes and I start to hear some stirring throughout the big house. Doors shutting and plates clattering. I wander out into the main room. Mr. Melancon is snoring baritone on the couch with all his clothes still on and his old dusty hat leaning over his eyes. Felix is in one of the big fluffy chairs and already rubbing his eyes. He nods at me.

"Sleep okay, kid?"

I look at him for a while but don't say anything. He sticks his finger in his ear and raises his eyebrows at me. "Still too young for coffee, I guess?" he asks, standing up.

I shrug my shoulders at him, sit down on the couch

and start to fiddle with my horn. A few minutes later, Mr. de Valencia wheels himself into the room and right over to me. He smiles at me, but I can tell that the smile may not be genuine at this point in time. Just like the smile that Louis used to give reporters when they asked him about something stupid like the *Soviet Union*, when all he wanted to do was make beautiful music that made people happy. I try to look at Mr. de Valencia with my own true smile, but I can't because I'm feeling guilty about the pistol that's in my backpack but that doesn't belong to me.

Mr. de Valencia clears his throat. "I spoke with a Mrs. Jones last night, Andre. I assume she would be your...stepmother? She was very, very upset when she called me last night. I'm sure you can understand. And I'm sure you are just as upset. How could you not be? We spoke at length, my boy. She said that...that the police were also upset. And I also felt upset when I heard about what happened when the officer tried to take your horn. We all talked about it. I know you didn't mean to punch that police officer, but it has made them quite upset."

I can see that Mr. Melancon is awake now, completely, and watching me with a very serious look on his face. Felix has come over too and he does look very upset as well, giving me one of the saddest looks I've ever seen.

"We talked and decided that the best thing would be for you to get a good night's sleep and in the morning, which is now, for us to take you downtown to the police station. Are you ready to go now, and to talk to the police?" Mr. de Valencia says.

I stare at him. This is how it's going to start. All three of them are looking at me with sad eyes, but they would never understand about what I'm thinking and feeling, because this is something even the best books can't explain, right in this moment. If they did understand, even just a little bit, they wouldn't be trying to take me downtown.

I shake my head no.

"Now, Andre," Mr. de Valencia says to me, "please try to understand. Put yourself in our shoes."

I want him to put himself in mine. Why can't he? He is a thoughtful man. I shake my head, harder this time.

Mr. de Valencia stops trying to explain, because I suppose he's at least thoughtful enough to know when he cannot. He reaches out and puts an arm on my shoulder and pats me three times.

"I'm so sorry, dear boy," he says. I see a small tear forming in the corner of his eye. He wheels himself away quickly and disappears from the room.

There's nothing else to do. I think about running again, but I am too tired, and I'm still not ready yet to be completely alone. I'm still afraid. So, I let them take me.

We go downtown in Mr. Melancon's old car, taking St. Charles and passing four different streetcars on the way. We also pass by the spot where I stood with Daddy on Fat Tuesday just a few weeks earlier, but now it's empty.

I'm sitting in the back seat holding my horn in my lap, trying not to see the streetcars.

"My father died last year," Felix says from the front, his eyes staying forward. I can't tell if he's saying it to me or not, but Mr. Melancon looks at him and shakes his head. There are plastic beads in every oak tree. I want to blow my horn so hard that my lips will split, but I don't do it. I just sit in the back of the car and go downtown. I put my horn in my backpack and zip it up tight.

The old scar on my neck starts to itch and burn, which it sometimes does when I get too anxious about something.

I've never liked downtown because there are too many bad sounds, even though it's fun to think that it was these same streets and sidewalks that little Louis lived his life on. I like to think it was sleepier back then. But not now. This time there's a great big garbage truck in front of us that squeals like it's dying every time it slows down. There are also bars with the doors open and, even though it's morning time, there are people yelling and acting foolish on the corners. Cars are honking their horns and playing music with only bass and no treble.

We pull into the parking lot of the police station. I know that's where we are because every single car in the parking lot is a police car. We go inside, and when I pass through the metal detector it goes crazy. I wait with my eyes closed for someone to discover that I have stolen a pistol and brought it into a place where you aren't supposed to, but it doesn't happen.

Instead, Mr. Melancon moves his coat aside and shows a big gun on his belt to the guard on duty, flashes some kind of a card in his wallet. The guard looks too heavy to get up from his seat, and so he just waves us all through and goes back to scrolling on his smartphone.

I realize then that both Mr. Melancon and Felix have guns on their belts, and that makes me feel less bad about having the one in my backpack, even though I stole it.

As I go through the building, I notice that there are beaucoup people looking at me—mostly ladies in business suits with big badges pinned to their chests and with cards dangling down by their sides. Some have pistols and some don't. When they see me, they stop what they're doing, look at me with a bunch of hangdog sadness, and whisper to one another in a way that I can certainly tell is about me. The men in the office seem to be the exact opposite. They can't look away fast enough, and I catch one or two of them that were leaning against a table shooting the breeze tighten up and start pretending to shuffle papers when me and the detectives stroll by.

At last, we come to a room with a big desk. Mr. Melancon says a few words to the police officer behind the desk, words that I can't quite make out. I wish that Mr. de Valencia had come with us. Now that they have me here, these police, I'm afraid of what they're going to do to me. Somehow I know that Mr. de Valencia wouldn't let any of that bad stuff happen, even though he can't even stand up from his wheel-chair. But he isn't here.

They bring me into an even smaller room, where they sit me down across a desk from a pretty lady with big, kind eyes. She smiles at me. Mr. Melancon whispers something into her ear and she nods her head, then he comes back around and puts a hand on my shoulder for just a second before quickly pulling it away.

"Hello there, Andre. My name is Janine. You doing alright, sugar?"

She waits for me to answer, but I don't. I try to smile at her to let her know that I'm not just being rude. But I can't really do it, so maybe I am.

"Can you tell me what happened?" Janine says.

When I don't answer, she looks over my shoulder to where Mr. Melancon is sitting.

"Doesn't say much," Mr. Melancon says.

"He likes music," Felix says.

Janine smiles at me again. I pull my horn out of my backpack and hold it tight in my lap. She looks down at it for a long time and then back up at me again.

"Can you tell me what you saw, on the streetcar? I know this must be a very hard time for you. But it's very important that you tell me what you saw. What happened?"

The streetcar. I feel myself start to lean. My lips purse up and tremble. I can feel a pressure behind my eyes. It is pushing and pushing. I'm looking out into the green tunnel of Carrolton Street. The cars are moving away. The people are moving away. Everything is getting smaller and it has already happened before I can stop it. Soon it's rushing away. I feel myself leaning even more.

"Andre, what happened on the streetcar?"

Louis Armstrong is just a poor boy. He needs his daddy. I can taste the copper in my mouth. Quarter notes beat in my heart. The gun is glowing hot against my back.

"Please, kid. You've got to answer her," a voice says behind me.

I try to open my mouth. I want to speak. But I can't. Nothing comes out. My eyes start to water. I slip out of the chair and I'm looking up at the fake, bright lights above me, getting all blurry. I hear feet shuffling around the room.

"Oh, child," Janine says and comes from behind the desk to put her arms around me. She hugs me to her big chest, where I stay, sobbing, for a long, long time.

FIVE

Melancon watched Janine embrace the boy. She held him for a while, letting him weep softly against her chest. One thing was for sure, this was about as much as they were going to get from the kid, and pressing him more and more just wasn't the right thing to do. It felt wrong, ham-handed, in poor form to even have him in here. The boy wasn't going to be opening up to anyone anytime soon, not any more than this, anyway. He needed to be with people who loved him.

After some time, Andre finally was back in his chair with a tissue, his big eyes blinking, while Janine looked down at him tenderly. "Felix, would you mind?" Melancon said, nodding his head towards the hallway. Felix understood, held a hand out for the boy, who took it and followed the young detective out of the room. The door closed softly behind them, and Janine's face changed instantly.

"First of all, David, where the *hell* has the boy been? He attacked a police officer last night, which was the same night he witnessed a homicide, mind you, and from there he was nowhere to be found. A dozen black-and-whites spent the night crawling all over Uptown looking for him. And then he just happens to turn up in your custody? Why is it that you're always tangled up in these things? Answer me that!"

He scooted his chair closer to her, though the wide desk kept the distance between them.

"Damn, Janine, do you know how many years it took me, back when I was a police detective, to get my own private office? I mean, at least two decades. You've been at it what? A year or two now? Look at this place. You done really well for yourself, and I know you deserve it."

She stared him down, narrowing her eyes and pinching up her lips.

"You could be charged with kidnapping, you know."

"Anybody can be charged with anything, Janine."

"So why don't you just tell me what happened? Exactly what happened. *No* creative license, David."

He sighed. "We've already been through it. Kid just showed up. He's a friend of Tomás. We got in touch with his stepmama, but she said she couldn't take him, asked us to babysit. Begged us, actually. We brought him straight here the next morning. What were we supposed to do? Take the kid straight downtown in the middle of the night covered in—"

"Covered in what, David?"

He hesitated. Stood up and knocked on the exterior door. Felix came in.

"Give her the shirt."

"Ah, right."

Felix took out a freezer bag with a little boy's shirt bundled tightly inside of it, the blackened bloodstains clearly visible through the clear plastic.

Janine stood up. "So now we can add tampering with evidence to your lists of charges," she said, snatching the freezer bag.

"We just delivered you the damn thing, now relax, Detective."

She brushed herself off, nodding and running her tongue along her teeth. Her eyes had gone drifting now across the pattern of blood on the shirt.

"Look," she said, putting it down and leaning against the desk. "The truth is, we've got nothing so far, except what you've just brought me. The witnesses scattered, the security camera caught pretty much nothing, and we've got a million and one prints, of course, because the crime scene is a damn century-old piece of public transport. And what's more—"

Felix spoke up then, raising his chin and interrupting the discussion.

"What's going to happen...to Andre?"

Janine turned and fiddled with some paperwork on the desk. "We're in touch with the Lashawn Jones, who's the one who should have custody...but...there's a problem. CPS may have to get involved. At least for the time being."

"CPS...Child Protective Services?"

"That's right," Janine said, now looking down at the floor.

"What's wrong with his mother?"

"It's his stepmother, actually, the one you claim to have talked to on the phone? She appears to have had some kind of psychotic break."

"No kidding?"

Janine nodded solemnly. "She has a brother she's appointed as temporary guardian, which doesn't sound like something a psychotic person would be capable of doing, to me. But I'm not a shrink, after all. It isn't a long-term solution, though. Either the stepmama has to get better and retain custody or..."

"Or he's going to be institutionalized... that's what you're telling me?" Melancon demanded angrily.

"It's a possibility, David."

Just then they could hear the sound of sneakers squeaking in the corridor. Janine walked over to the door and stuck her head out.

SIX

He didn't shoot anyone. Not Louis. That's why he had such a hard time to begin with, I think—because he was a *gentle soul*. Like me. Angry, scared, but gentle. Some books even go so far as to say that the pistol he stole from his stepdaddy's trunk was loaded with blanks. I don't know about that, but I do know that if he had accidentally shot someone, you would have never known his name.

No International Airport, no King of Zulu, no Carnegie Hall.

But he didn't. He just shot the air.

Blam, blam, blam.

Right into the night sky, sending the other children scattering. Did he laugh? Or did he frighten himself? I don't know. But maybe he felt less scared, if only for a second or two.

What happened next is that police officers rushed

towards him on horseback, guns already drawn. Guns pointed at him, not at the sky. Little Louis Armstrong dropped the pistol on the banquette as the cops on Clydesdales charged towards him (clop clop clop). *What have I done?* he thought to himself. Louis screamed when the thick arms seized him. He wailed. He cried. He'd be in the paper the next day for his crime. That was the first time his name would ever show up in the paper, but far from the last.

If things were hard before, they were about to get much, much harder. Now, Louis is a criminal. And if the world hates a poor daddy-less boy from back of town, it hates one that breaks the law even more so. He has no idea that being arrested on New Year's for firing his stepdaddy's pistol is going to be one of the luckiest things that ever happens to him.

That it is *destiny*.

So, Louis screams and cries with his Big Dipper mouth, wailing and rolling on the nasty street. If he had done this just a few years later, it would have been incredibly unlucky, because the judge would have sent a grown man straight to penitentiary. As it stood, though, Louis was just the right age.

My age.

So, the judge sent little Louis to a place called the Colored Waif's Home for Boys.

I wonder if Louis, hearing the judge's notion, had to pause and think about what the word *waif* meant, because *I* had to look it up in the dictionary. I'm glad I did, though, because it turns out that *I am now a waif* as well. So, a good word to know about, I guess.

I'm sitting in the hallway of the police station, thinking about my waif life to come. A janitor is trying to mop, but when he sees me, he drags the wet thing to the other end of the hall. Squeak squeak go his shoes.

When the mop man moves out of the way, that's when I see Uncle. I dry my eyes as quick as I can with the little tissue in my hand and then I toss the whole snotty mess in the trash. Uncle is coming down the hallway fast towards me. I know the way he walks, even before I'm able to make out his face. He's got an officer behind him, that blue shape strutting and jangling like it owns the whole joint. But Uncle's walk is so different from that he stands out like a broken guitar string. He is wide-legged, smooth-moving, muscly at the top and thin around the waist. His long braids sway in the bright light and his shoes squeak too.

"Hey, little man," he says to me when he gets to where I'm sitting. He doesn't smile but he puts a hand on my shoulder and squeezes, bends down low and looks me right in the eyes. "You making it?"

The door to the room has come open now and the detectives are spilling out.

"Felix Herbert," Felix says, and he shakes Uncle's hand.

"Melph. I'm this young'un's uncle. I'm here to pick him up."

"So we were told," Mr. Melancon says and grins real big at Uncle, but I can see that his blue eyes are not grinning but rather watching real close.

I stand up and take Uncle Melph's hand. As we start to walk away, I turn to look back at the detectives. Mr. Melancon and Felix stand there in the hallway watching me go, looking sad.

I wave at them. A few seconds pass where I think maybe they won't wave back, but they do—just as I'm turning the corner, they wave back.

I guess I forgive them for taking me downtown. Daddy always said it was good to forgive.

A few minutes later and Uncle is gently buckling me into the passenger seat of his Explorer. He watches my face real close while he's doing it. I've taken my horn out of my bag again and am holding it tight in my lap and we're going up Claiborne Avenue. He's fiddling with the radio, asking me what I'm listening to these days. We pass by groups of men out on the neutral ground playing dominoes and checkers on the top of cardboard boxes. I look out of the window and watch the top of the Superdome, all glinting in the sunlight, as it gets smaller and smaller.

"You know your Mama Jones, she ain't well," he says, while we're stopped at a red light and looking at the long line out in front of a chicken shop. "I'm not sure if she's going to be alright or not. She's taking it real hard. She might not be okay."

The light turns green.

"Are you?" he asks me, without turning his head.

I look at him, my lower lip starting to tremble again.

"You going to have to go on and be the man of the house now, little Andre. Be strong for her."

I can't help it, not being strong. Someone is either strong or they aren't, and I'm not. The tears are pushing out from somewhere that's almost not a part of me at all. The same feeling as where the wind comes from when I blow a high C on the horn. Some of the things that come out of me just come, and I don't call them. I can't stop them either.

"You know when I was in Iraq, and stuff got real bad, we couldn't have no one next to us crying and carrying on and having a breakdown. Not when things got real bad like that. Got real bad like they're getting right now. Now is when you have to have one of those stone-faced sonofabitches right next to you. One of those people that can just push it all the way down and carry on. Do you understand what I mean, young'un?"

Maybe I do, but it doesn't matter to me, not right now.

"Don't start crying. You're going to have a tough time, and you got to be tough in turn."

But I can't stop my lip, or the wetness leaking from

my face. So, I just turn away and try to think about Louis Armstrong. I Think about his wide face smiling up at the lights, his lips pressed against the mouthpiece, his white handkerchief swinging.

"Mama Jones might be going away for a while. To the hospital. And with your daddy gone, you going to stay with me for a while in the extra bedroom. We're going to have a good time. You can blow your horn all you want."

He takes a corner a little too fast, and I can feel my weight shift to the side of the car.

"You going to be alright, Andre. You going to have to grow up fast, though. It is time for you to be a man now."

A pothole makes the car bounce. We're up into the Seventeenth Ward now, almost up onto Leonidas, where Melph lives. I get a sick feeling in my stomach. I don't know if it's the car ride or the different food Mr. de Valencia gave me or the trip downtown, but I don't feel very well at all suddenly.

I notice that Melph is looking at me real close, down at my neck, at my scar.

"You remember how you got that scar, Andre?"

I shake my head.

"You don't remember, right?"

I shake my head again, feeling the sickness come over me and not able to wait any longer.

He pulls over and I open the door and puke right

out on the curb. Uncle reaches over and pats me on the back a few times before putting his hands back on the wheel.

"So, you were on the streetcar. With your daddy?" he says once I'm sitting back straight and wiping my lips with my shirtsleeve.

I nod my head.

Uncle looks far down the street and squints his eyes. His fingers are so long on the steering wheel. Huge hands, he's got, like a piano player. But he doesn't play an instrument.

"And you saw him, when he..." Uncle isn't looking at me.

I'm happy the cold brass is between my fingers. I hug the horn to my chest.

"Damn...," Uncle says and shakes his head from side to side, slapping the steering wheel lightly with those long, long hands (smack, smack).

I want to say *damn*.

Damn. Damn. Damn.

"You didn't see who did it, though?" Uncle asks.

When I don't answer, he nods his head towards the house—*orange soda bungalow* is how Daddy always described Melph's place.

"Come on in and play me a tune, then, nephew," he says.

I DON'T HAVE to wonder what Louis Armstrong might have done, if he were in my shoes right now, because I know exactly what he did. I know it because it's right there in the books, in black and white. It has already happened. It happened so long ago that now it's just a few lines, just a few words even, and so it seems so small when you read about it. But what's happening to me right now doesn't seem small, not at all. Am I going to be okay? I don't think so. The things up ahead are invisible for me. But with Louis, you can flip the pages back and forth, and he always does the same thing. For some reason, thinking of that makes me feel safe, or safer at least. I wonder if there will ever be a book about my life and if it's too late to change what will be written inside of it.

It's a few hours later, and the sky has gone from blue to red to purple and now to black outside of the window. I'm in the back of the house, in the bedroom thrown together for me. It's mostly weights back here, an exercise bike, all of it moved off into the closet now to make way for me, I guess. My futon with the broken springs has laundry piled up on it and the floor sags in one corner where all of the heavy dumbbells were kept before, a layer of dust on everything.

Mama Jones always said her brother Melph was too handsome to ever have a wife, but I think it might be because he's too messy.

I dump out my bag. There's the gun and my horn

63

lying on the futon side by side. I take a few deep breaths, think for a while, and then put them both back carefully.

There's also a big mirror in the center of the wall, and I catch my reflection in it. I stare at myself for a long, long time, listening to the music of the neighborhood around me. Dogs bark and women laugh, motorcycles churn and I can even hear the streetcar bell, only just softly. It still hurts just as much. The train by the river howls out at about seven o'clock, and things get a bit quieter after that.

Mirrors are one of my least favorite things, especially in the last year or two, but I can't look away. My legs have gotten longer. There's fuzzy hair on my chin. My lips are busted and there's a small ring around my mouth just like the one that worried Louis his whole life. My hair is dirty and my eyes are red. The slim scar on my neck is pale and forked.

I break the mirror's spell and wander around the house a bit. Uncle has gone off somewhere, and he never said where he was going or what time he'd be back. He left a few slices of pizza on the kitchen table for me, covered in a paper towel. I take a bite and chew it up a bit before starting to feel sick all over again. But I realize also how badly my body wants the pizza, even if my brain doesn't. I haven't eaten much in the last two days, so I force myself to finish a whole piece.

From the kitchen table I can see the door to

Uncle's bedroom, which for some reason is this very particular shade of red. There is something about that red, though I couldn't say just what. The door is also slightly open and there's a light left on inside, which is very mysterious looking in the way it dimly shines out just a bit onto the wall opposite. Something about the red door, the light, the pizza churning in my stomach, makes me stand up and walk over. Then I stand by the door for a long while, looking at it and just thinking.

I push it open and it whines on its hinges, walk inside until I'm standing over Uncle's bed. There are moving boxes spilling open on the floor, like they were packed too quickly. I wonder where Uncle is moving to. There are empty bottles on his dresser, pills, condoms, and—

Something else. Something I felt like was there, though I couldn't have said how I knew or why or what brought me in here. But then I realize.

The lipstick is a certain color, that certain shade of red, same as the door. The tube of it has been left open and sits on a tissue that's also marked with the color. The smudge of muddy red sends a funny feeling up into my stomach and I stare for a long time.

Marsala. That's the weird name for the weird color. Where did that word just pop into my head from? I don't know how I remember the name, but I will never forget the color. I think because it looks like a certain kind of wine. *Marsala lipstick.*

Why is this here? This marsala lipstick sitting on the edge of Uncle Melph's dresser, left open, left on a tissue?

I back out of the room, go and get my backpack and zip it up.

Louis Armstrong didn't know it yet, but his whole life was about to start.

The pistol he shot into the night sky. It's just a few lines in a book. But they sent him to become a waif, and it was the best thing that could ever have happened to him. It may have saved his life.

I take a green bandana from Uncle's workout clothes in my room and I tie it around my head. Then I take his old army jacket from off a hook in the hall and put it on. I've stolen three things today already, after having gone thirteen years resisting.

But I'm a waif now. I have to do what I have to do. The jacket's a little big for me, but I know that it'll be cold where I'm going.

I leave. I walk right out the front door.

The street in front of me is empty and stretches all the way down to the vanishing point.

SEVEN

Tomás was sitting on the wide front porch, watching the evening go by on the Avenue, and hating himself with a passion.

A young man, a child really, had come to this address looking for help. A boy had fled from trauma and trusted Tomás on the worst, most difficult night of his life.

And what had Tomás done?

He had summarily sent the poor boy downtown. Turned him over to the uncouth authorities, to the state. Washed his hands of the whole matter in time for breakfast. What kind of a man would do such a thing?

His honor, quite clearly, had been sullied by this failure.

But what else was a man to do? How to again hold his head up high? He was old, burdened by this damned chair. A murder had taken place, after all. The boy was a witness. And who was Tomás to—

He should have done more, that much he was sure of.

Now he felt weak, helpless, the weight of the chair suddenly seeming so absolute and terrible. Tomás, on this troubled night, was having no luck savoring the small beauties of a moonlit avenue. He sighed into an iced tea, clearly picturing all the horrors that must lie before little Andre, the boy's whole future flashing in terrible vividness before his imagination's eye, all of it pivoting around that crucial moment: a moment in which Tomás had failed to summon the courage to—

"To what, exactly?" he said to the swaying crepe myrtles. "To kidnap a traumatized child for his own good? To keep a witness hostage from the detectives who need to interrogate him? To insert myself into a terrible family tragedy?"

The trees held no answer. But Tomás knew better, and now all that was left was to sit here and torture himself over this shortcoming. He must sit and wait with these damned thoughts, wait for the detectives to return with some news.

News that would surely be of the unhappy variety.

Tomás brought himself and his chair inside, looked longingly at the old gramophone that Andre had been so fond of. The Louis Armstrong record was still there. He wheeled a bit closer and stared down at the round piece of petroleum, set the needle on it and turned it on.

Halfway through the second song—the syrupy sweet and doleful "West End Blues," which mirrored the old man's feelings with a stirring precision—there was a knock on the door, launching Tomás out of his reverie instantly. He lifted the needle from the player, straightened his tie.

"You don't have to knock, Felix. This is your home too, you know," Tomás called out, his voice bouncing around the grand manor.

The young detective walked into the parlor and was followed closely behind by Melancon, who wore lines on his face even deeper than usual. Both of them collapsed on the couch.

"Tell me everything," Tomás demanded.

Melancon shook his head. "Nothing. The boy wouldn't say a word. Wouldn't or...maybe couldn't. I'm still not sure which. I still haven't heard the kid open his mouth."

Tomás, usually the type to listen more than he spoke, could scarcely hold his tongue. He had so many questions.

"Imagine, the only witness to a murder case, unable to talk," Melancon said.

Tomás looked at the ceiling, trying to recall exactly what he'd been told upon taking the boy under his wing a few months earlier. He wanted to get it right.

"I'm no psychologist," Tomás finally began, "but I believe it's not that he is unable to talk to people. His words to me have been single ones. He will smile and say 'good' or 'nice' after a song. So, he clearly has the ability to speak. In fact, I think it might be appropriate to simply say that he is just a very quiet person. Tell me, how was he received at the station? Were they kind?"

Felix poured himself some of the tea from the pitcher on the coffee table, leaned back into the couch and downed it in one gulp. "Just quiet?" he asked, smacking his lips a bit. "I thought maybe that scar on his neck was from some sort of surgery, that it had maybe wrecked his cords. You said you'd heard him say a few words, though?"

"After some time," Tomás replied, "mostly in response to the gramophone. I believe he therefore has no physical limitations on his speech, but that he speaks only when thoroughly comfortable, and even then, he remains a boy of few words. Due to the current situation, the stresses placed on him, the trauma, I doubt if he will speak for some time. Though I am sure that he could speak at length if he wished to. He is a very fast learner and has always seemed to me to be highly, highly intelligent. He has a deep appreciation for music, and to hear him blow that horn of his, *Dios mío*. Now tell me, how did you leave it with the police?"

"A strange kid," Melancon said absently.

Tomás shook his head. "I'm just beside myself, gentlemen. Tell me what happened precisely, and tell me this instant! I feel a great deal of guilt and sadness, and I feel as if I have brought a great dishonor onto our house. He is a fine young man, and now to be without a father, to come to us for help only to be turned away."

"It gets worse," Melancon said. He and Felix exchanged a long look of despair. Felix turned his palms up and cocked his head, the way he always did before issuing an apology. His shoulders drooped and he looked Tomás in the eye.

"Kid's mother was...well, she was obviously very upset with the whole thing. Apparently, she may be...institutionalized."

"Stepmama?"

"Oh, right."

"Where is his real mother?"

Melancon shrugged. "I'm not sure."

"So, what happened? With the stepmom? Mrs. Jones?" Tomás pressed.

"Well, she was refusing to leave the house to identify her husband's body. When they tried to make her leave, apparently, she went a little nutso. I was told there were a few dishes thrown. Maybe understandable, given her condition. But it looks like Child Protective Services may be getting involved. For now, the kid has been released into the custody of an uncle."

Tomás quietly bowed his head while he turned all of this over in his mind. With one hand he gently rocked his wheelchair forward and back. With the other he worried his hairy chin, his substantial eyebrows scrunched into the center of his forehead.

"Well...I suppose you would have already told me if there was news regarding the killer of Andre's father?" he asked flatly.

"All we know is that it was a bullet," Melancon said, leaning forward. "There were only a few people on the streetcar, and none of them have come forward yet as witnesses. Downtown says the security footage is worthless. And other than that, zilch. Except for the boy, of course."

"He saw everything?" Tomás asked.

"Only he knows the answer to that question, and nobody is sure how to get it out of him."

Tomás deflated. "So young, to see such a thing. I wish I could have helped him more. But I am old. I am in this damned chair." He slapped the metal seat beneath him, gnashing his teeth a bit as he did so.

"There's nothing for it, old friend," Felix said. Melancon nodded, taking his hat in his hands and standing up from the couch.

"You did everything you could, Tomás," the old detective said. "I know how you feel. Seeing a kid like that, kind of helpless, you want to take him under your wing. Hell, you can still help him down the road. But for right now, all you can do is stand down."

The two detectives stuck around for another cup, all three men trying to delicately avoid the subject so clearly troubling their minds, taking comfort in each other's company. They let the Armstrong record play quietly from the corner.

Just as Tomás was about to broach the subject of supper, a strange sound.

It was not unlike the bleating of a trumpet, only muffled somehow. Not the real thing, but some kind of a recording, and a hampered one at that. They could only just hear it below the record. It sounded something like a horn with a sock stuffed in it coming from three feet underground. At first, all three men simply stood up and looked about. Melancon killed the record. Eyebrows were raised and necks turned this way and that.

"The hell is that?" Felix finally said.

Two minutes went by and none of them could locate the source of the strange sound. It would stop and then start anew, just loud enough to keep them looking, but just faint enough so that its source refused to be pinpointed. They looked behind potted plants and the framed photographs on the shelves. Felix bent under furniture, finally finding the rattling thing underneath the fluffy cushion of the round-armed sofa with the floral pattern.

A phone. It buzzed and again, the long peal of a trumpet solo now unmistakable as the ring tone. They all looked at it. Felix held it out in front of himself like it was a foreign relic before he was jogged by his ever-curious partner.

"Well, answer it," Melancon said.

Felix did so, sliding his pointer finger across the screen and pressing the button that engaged the speaker-phone.

"Hello," he said.

A rough but musical voice answered. "Who is this?" it demanded.

"Felix Herbert."

A silence.

"You the man from the police station? The one that brought in Andre?"

A long pause. Everyone waited before the voice continued.

"You got my nephew?"

Melancon pointed to the phone, as if that would somehow clarify the situation. But Felix had already picked up the thread.

"Is this...Melph...is this Andre's uncle?"

"Yeah."

"Wait a minute...now, I thought you had taken

Andre. I thought you took him from the station, that he was released into your custody."

"I did...but he's...well, he isn't here anymore. I've been texting him for an hour, because...well you know...he doesn't talk. Not even to answer a call. Not even in an emergency. Damn boy can be a lot of trouble sometimes. But I don't know what else to do."

Another long and awkward pause. Tomás covered his face with his hands and hung his head low.

"So, you don't have Andre?" Felix tried.

"Well, wait a minute, you got his damn phone. So, where's *he* at?"

The anger in the voice caused Felix to hesitate. His eyes ping-ponged between the two older men before he finally answered. "Yes, we have his phone. We just found it. Under the couch cushions. Andre must have dropped it when—"

"So, you haven't seen him?" Melph said. "Damn!"

He then began mumbling apologies, in stark contrast to the accusatory tone of a moment before. Tomás made an uncertain gesture at the young detective, who made one back.

Tomás wheeled himself over and grabbed the phone from Felix, putting his mouth up close to the receiver. "This is Tomás de Valencia. Do you mean to tell us that you have lost the poor child, after he was entrusted to you?"

Felix pulled the phone away and covered the receiver, making a silencing motion at his old friend.

"Look, never mind," Melph said. "This is between us in the family anyway. Just...mail me his phone, would you? 4533 Leonidas."

Melancon made a quick note on his notepad. "Wait a minute, can you tell me—" the old detective shouted as he leaned into the phone, but the clicking sound emanating from the receiver was unmistakable: the call was over.

"Gentlemen, this just continues to grow worse and worse!" Tomás cried in the dead silence that followed. "Now the poor child is lost...lost in this Gomorrah with no one by his side. Unable or unwilling to speak. Without a phone...without any money." As he said these words, he seemed to wheel himself backwards, inch by unconscious inch, retreating from the entire dark ordeal.

Felix twiddled with the phone a bit, finally collapsing on the couch with one of his trademark sighs of exasperation. He got himself comfortable and began to pore over the device, inspecting contacts and notifications, scrolling through history, even checking what videos the boy had watched.

Melancon took a step closer to Tomás. "Where would he go?" the old detective asked.

"Where do young boys go when they run away from home?" Tomás replied, a rhetorical shrug to his shoulders and a dreadful despondency in his voice. "He came *here* the last time he was in need, but after the way I treated him, I doubt he'll ever make that mistake a second time."

"There is no sense in beating yourself up any more than you already have," Felix said from the couch. "He came here because you were his friend, and you acted in the only way that was possible."

"Back in my day we'd go to the river," Melancon said, walking over to finger the gramophone. "Maybe to the racetrack. These days I've got no idea."

"Was this before or after you ended up in a Norman Rockwell painting, partner?"

Melancon crossed his arms and raised an eyebrow at Felix. "All we know is that the kid likes music. And that isn't much to go on. It's a big city, and if there's one thing it's full to the brim with, besides water and potholes, its music."

"Let me remind you gentlemen that while you are quipping back and forth, there is a child, a child who witnessed a horrendous crime, mind you, out on the streets!" Tomás said. "He is but a boy and has seen something that no child should have to see. And I have certain dark fears and imaginings about what comes next if we tarry too long."

"You don't think he can make it?" Felix asked.

"It is not the street smarts of young master Andre that concern me, Felix. What I fear the most is that the person who committed the murder, to which he may be the only witness, may still linger on those same streets. And I should certainly not have to tell you, detectives, what that could mean."

Melancon picked up the jacket of the old Louis Armstrong record, which showed the iconic trumpeter with cheeks inflated like eight balls, eyes turned upwards, his white handkerchief draped in his playing hand. "To someone out there, someone particularly violent, this boy is a huge liability."

Tomás nodded. "I need you to find him. Because this situation...it is a black mark on all of our souls. We can't trust this to the police. It's time for you to do the most important detective work of your lives. Find him and bring him here where we can protect him, and let us not fail him a second time. We'll sort the details out later, but I simply cannot abide that thought of something else terrible happening to that young boy on top of what he's already been through."

Felix stood up from the couch, slipping the phone into his coat pocket. "We'll find him," the young detective said.

Melancon laid the record sleeve back down near the gramophone.

"Yes, we will."

EIGHT

Louis the waif is standing on a curb and he's not the only one—he's there with a group of the other waifs, and all of them are just hungry. It's got nothing to do with food. It's the kind of hungry you get from being a waif. The kind of hungry you either understand from living it, or you just don't. It doesn't translate into any word. Like a lot of things, you just can't tell the feeling to someone unless they've felt it themselves, even though the books do try.

I know what it feels like, though, because I'm standing on the same cold streets as he did.

The waifs are supposed to be picking up trash. Mr. Peter Davis, one of the head honchos at the Colored Waif's Home for Boys, brought them there to do just that. But he is only one man and the waifs are many. He can't be a real daddy to thirty different boys, though he tries his best and does an okay job at being one-thirtieth a daddy to each and every one of them.

So, the waifs run around the neighborhood like a school of fish in a frenzy, like piranha on the nature channel. They punch and claw each other. On one corner, a mealy apple has fallen off a cart. The first boy to discover it is immediately piled on by the others until his lip is bloodied and he drops the fruit. The apple goes *poof* in a storm of hungry mouths and the kids leave off down the street.

Another corner brings another chance. Here, a man exits one of the *Prostitution establishments* (that's what the books call them, and that's what Storyville is most famous for, aside from Louis Armstrong, of course—but he doesn't know that yet, being just a waif). The children spot the fine gentleman, with his tailored suit and watch chain and top hat, and immediately begin to swarm. They jostle and push, each one of them already beginning to tap and twist. They bow and gyrate and wrestle, twisting their hungry muscles around on the old cobblestone streets. The hunger has taught them to dance as well. The hunger has taught them music.

But little Louis gets an edge somehow. Somehow, he manages to push the others off into the background. Because he is the star of this place. He doesn't know it yet, but he is. He finally pushes through the swarm of hungry bodies and then it's all Louis, center stage. He smiles that big smile and looks up with those wet eyes in a way that will later charm the whole world. He shakes his head and his limbs swing and he lets out a few nonsense scat sounds. "Zap doobie do whop," he sings, and then he bows really low to the gentleman, who at first was annoyed but now can't help himself but love Louis in a way that everyone will. Someday. But Louis doesn't know it yet. He doesn't know that he will show this to the world, this hungry music of empty bellies. All he knows is fear. Love has to get in the back of the line for now.

The gentleman smiles down at this charming little boy. He scoops a handful of shiny coins out of his jangling pocket. He grins again at Louis and then tosses them down into the street. Because even though he loves Louis, he thinks himself too high to stop and place a coin in a waif's hand. So, he dumps them down on the cobble and moves on.

There is a moment, with all of those hungry boys standing around with their eyes sharklike looking down at the shining coins. They all know it's every waif for himself, but it takes them a minute to get over the shock of seeing such an *embarrassment of riches* scattered all over the grime and muck of a Storyville street.

When the shock wears off a bit, they attack. They scramble and fumble and punch and even bite each other to get at the precious doubloons. They don't know that this is still the Louis show, and he is quicker than the lot of them, maybe because he's the hungriest and most daddy-less of them all, or maybe because he's powered by all the future world-love that will one day find him.

Louis scoops up the lion's share of coins. He has them in his fist. Now all the boys stare at him with their hungry eyes. The street has quieted down now. If this was an old western movie, a tumbleweed might have gone by just then. But this is not a western movie, it's real life for Louis.

The boys form a circle around him. They are edging closer and closer, tighter and tighter, cracking their knuckles and baring their teeth. It is their hunger against Louis and his hunger. Little Louis has the coins pressed in a tight little ball in his fist. He knows he will never hold on to them, or to anything else, if he lets the other waifs have this silver.

So, what does he do?

He puts them right in his mouth. The whole handful of coins, scooped up off of the dirty street—he pops them right in on his tongue, then sloshes them down between his lip and lower teeth and shuts his jaw tight like a trap.

The boys watch him in horror. *What would that taste like?* they wonder. A few of the hungrier boys even knock Louis down and take a chance trying to pull that mouth open. But they can't. Louis's lips are already as rough as burlap. They are strong and muscular. They are tight and do not release the treasure.

He gets up and brushes himself off, all that moola still bulging out of his lower lip.

One of the older boys slaps him across the face. Not too hard, but more as a show.

"Boy got a mouth like a damn satchel," the bully says and walks away like the fox did from the sour grapes.

The smaller waifs laugh at that, grinning.

"Satchel mouth, satchel mouth, satchel mouth!" they chant.

But for a few of the waifs, that's just too many syllables. None of them have been to school, or etiquette lessons on how to speak properly and *enunciate*. So, one of them shortens "satchel mouth" in a way that will echo out from Storyville forever.

"Satchmo, Satchmo, Satchmo," the boys chant.

I look at the different blocks I walk by, wondering which corner it happened on. But too much time has passed, and all of the old buildings have been cleared away for decades, and the books just don't say for sure. A long time ago the three bullets that Louis fired fell back to earth and buried themselves into something so deep that no one ever found them. I know this somehow, but I can't say why.

I think about the gun that is riding in the bottom of

my backpack, and it makes me feel ten percent less afraid than I would otherwise. But with it also comes a different kind of fear. There is something attached to the heavy piece of metal that I can't describe with words, but when I feel the hardness of it bounce against my lower back, I know that everything that happens now is important, more important than the future can ever be. I know that *this* will be the story they tell about me, if they tell any stories at all.

My feet are starting to cramp and ache because I couldn't take the streetcar. Not anymore. I tried. For almost an hour I stood under the branches at Audubon Park, standing in the shadow that hid my face, and I watched every car that drove by. I even saw the car with the chipped bell, now being driven by a different conductor. That hurt me so bad I nearly doubled over with the pain of it. It hurts still. I could make out the faces of every driver and I was looking for one that didn't know who I was. But every driver that passed by was one that would certainly recognize me, that would ask me question after question about my father, and if I didn't answer they would be likely to grab me and the whole situation would only repeat itself again and again. So, I walk, and I feel a sense of relief for not having to get on a streetcar again anyway.

It took me almost two hours to make it to here, and I wonder if my feet will start to bleed. The kicks I'm wearing are mostly worn-out trash, shoes that other kids in the Seventeenth would be embarrassed to wear. I would be embarrassed to wear them too, except I don't have many friends my age to feel embarrassed about.

The gate is shut because it's almost ten o'clock at night now. A homeless-looking man shuffles down the opposite side of the street from me. He's going real slow and keeping one of his eyes on me, but I pretend not to notice. I'm pretty much homeless too now—that's the thought that passes through my mind while I'm looking at him. Otherwise, the street is dead quiet. It's getting a bit cold, so I zip up Uncle Melph's army jacket, but I have to roll up the sleeves because I still need my hands.

I can see him standing there, on the other side of the gate, in Congo Square. His wide midsection, the horn hanging down at his side.

I've never been a good climber, but I've come too far now and there's no turning back. I throw my backpack up and over the top and jump as high as I can, grabbing the top of the fence. I scramble my bad shoes against the wrought-iron until the rubber soles get a grip on it, and then I'm up and over and sprawled out next to my backpack on the sacred ground before I realize what has happened.

Congo Square.

I listen really close for a park ranger or police officer to come rushing towards me, or maybe for some alarm to sound, but none of that happens. This is just a patch of dirt, after all.

It is a special one, though, one filled with ghosts and stories. This is where the slaves made jazz music. And when I sit up, I can see *him* standing in the middle of it all, or his outline anyway. He's the lord of it. There's some kind of a light behind him, palm fronds framing him where he stands, leaning slightly forward, his handkerchief at the ready.

The moon is fat up in the sky, pink and dreamy, and I can see just fine. It means that other people will be able to see me also, so I have to be a little careful not to let them. I take off low along one hedgerow, crouching and hiding, wondering if Uncle's camouflage jacket will help me at all.

I creep around for a few minutes, getting closer to the center of things. But then I start to worry about something else. I start to realize that there is not a soul here, no late-night security guard or sleepy park ranger. No one is here at all except for me and him, and then maybe a few old slave ghosts. I go from being scared of being caught to being scared of the place itself. Maybe I know why there are no people here, why they shut the gate up tight when the sun goes down. It's because even rangers are afraid to be around this place in the night. This is one of those places in the city that the spirits trouble. A place just like Storyville, which was only a few blocks away before it got torn down. I try to be brave. I have my gun, my horn, and now I have *him*, too.

I come out from behind a bush, deciding to just stand up and walk up to him like normal. Because there he is, waiting for me. Now I see him in close up, standing straight with that pink moon rising right above his head.

He's looking down at me, or at least it seems like. I don't know what he is made of. Maybe bronze or something like that. Maybe it's the same stuff that Andrew Jackson is made of down in *his* square.

He has his rag in one hand. A rag carved out of bronze, or whatever. He always carried it with him when he went on stage to wipe away the big drops of sweat that would come on his forehead, would trickle down his inflated cheeks, would *condensate* on his brass and sop his starched shirt. That sweat was just a part of it because he always put work into that mouthpiece. He'd put everything. He'd split his lips wide open on a high note and come out from under the lights all splattered in blood. He would come away from the stage looking like he'd just built a pyramid, just escaped, just saved the world. And maybe he had.

In his other hand is his trumpet. It's hung way down at his side, like he isn't even thinking about blowing it right at this moment because he's so relaxed to be just standing in his park, standing in Congo Square and looking down at *me*.

He's wearing fancy metal clothes and he even has a metal tie. Calm but serious. I stare at him right in his metal eyes, and I think about who he reminds me of most of all.

"Louis," I say.

I think maybe his eyes widen, the metal brows stretching under the moon. It looks like maybe they do.

"Louis."

He's waiting for the question, though.

"I'm scared."

I realize it still isn't a question, and his eyes look less warm than they did a moment before. He's here all day every day, but somehow I can still see that he's impatient for it. I hear tires squeal somewhere out on Basin Street.

"My daddy."

But Louis's metal lips still don't move. Not really. I stare at them so long that I think they might start to.

But no. He just stares. His face is round and black and hard like a cast-iron skillet. His eyes are narrow metal holes.

I'm talking to a statue. I know it. I'm not crazy, but I just can't stop.

"I saw him die."

Still nothing.

"I ain't like you, Louis. What should I do?"

No answer. The statue only watches forever. I wish I was made of metal. I look over the top of his head at the lights of the tall buildings, at the clouds rolling in between them.

A sound. Finally.

I look back at Louis, but he still hasn't moved. He hasn't raised his horn to his lips, but I swear I can hear jazz music. If I was in a boat on the ocean and someone played that music from the sandy bottom of the sea, I would know just what it was. And that's what I hear now, coming from someplace far away.

Music. Good music. Great music, even.

Is it just in my head? Am I crazy?

Louis still hasn't moved, but the sound is coming from somewhere off behind him, real. Must be. It's bouncing down one of the long streets that lead to his park from all sides, from one of many old paths that lead right here to Congo Square.

Louis winks one of his big bronze eyes right at me. I could swear it.

A trombone.

A tuba.

A snare drum.

I hear them getting louder and closer. I know now that they're coming down from somewhere in the neighborhood. The big sound. Instruments distinct, separate, no melody.

I move towards that sound before I can think of all the reasons why I shouldn't.

NINE

The next morning broke with one of those brilliant spring sunrises in South Louisiana—dewy and green and windswept, the swampy miasma all blown away.

But Melancon wasn't working with enough sleep to appreciate the glorious way it dawned.

He and Felix had spent a tense night driving all over the city. They'd begun in the Seventeenth Ward and woven eastward up and down from river to lake, completing the circumnavigation six times. It had been nearly three in the morning when they'd finally agreed to call it off, the aching tiredness overcoming their guilt and the promises made. By then the El Camino had a deflated tire from all the Orleans Parish potholes, and Melancon himself had a sore back from the same. He'd been so achy and stiff that he had actually gone home to his dingy room in St. Roch, just to sleep in an actual bed.

Not a single sign of Andre, Melancon thought to himself, walking up the dimly lit stairs to his office. The boy must be a damn magician as well as a trumpet player. Andre the magnificent. Either that or something far worse had happened: something that Melancon wasn't ready to imagine just yet. Two or three times in the dark night, they had stopped young men who fit the description from a distance, and each time been disappointed by a surprised stranger's face gawking back at them, decidedly less than silent about being approached in such a way.

It was now six thirty, and despite the late night, the two detectives were already yawning and sipping coffee together as the sun peeked over the tops of the old buildings and through the French doors of the Basin Street Detective Agency. Felix, though still in his twenties, had dark circles under his eyes, greasy hair, and a noticeable droop to his shoulders. Melancon shuddered to think what he himself must look like with forty-some years added to the equation and quietly made up his mind to avoid mirrors for the day. The old detective pulled his fedora brim as low as he could, breathing in the steam from his cup.

"You peg Andre to be street-savvy?" Felix asked through a yawn, thoughtfully stirring some heavy cream into the darkness of his mug.

Melancon had already considered the question some on last night's long car ride, which had taken them through some less-than-favorable areas of the city, and was ready with his diagnosis. "Well, we know the neighborhood he's from on the one hand. There has to be a little toughness to him, or he wouldn't have made it growing up there. On the other hand, kid is thirteen, and saying he's a bit of an oddball would be generous. He's a weird guy, and weird guys get picked on a lot, get seen as easy targets. All I know is that if he isn't street-smart, then we had better start looking harder, because he won't last long alone wherever he is. If he *is* street-smart, we might as well give up because we probably won't find him at all if he doesn't want to be found."

"Damn, do you have to be such an optimist all the time, Melancon?"

The old detective shrugged.

"Sounds like we're fucked either way," Felix said.

Melancon shrugged again for good measure, as it was about all he had the energy to do until he got the coffee down. "We've been here before," he said and took the biggest gulp of brew the heat of it would allow, feeling his bones shiver with exhaustion.

"A kid without language like that...I can't...I mean...that puts him at a big disadvantage, doesn't it?" Felix went on. "Even if he is as sharp as Tomás says."

Melancon raised his eyebrows. "Might be better for a kid like that *not* to talk too much. People might get the idea that he's a hard screw. Silence says a lot on its own, you know."

"I bet you never dodged a scrape that way."

The old detective painfully straightened his back. "My tongue gets me out of trouble, most of the time, by wagging, not by sitting still."

"You mean the same trouble it just got you in?"

"You aren't exactly what I'd call a *silent partner* either, Felix."

The young man knocked his knuckles against the hardwood desk and glanced up at the clock on the wall.

"So, what's next, then?" he asked. "Because if we just sit here, I'll fall asleep."

Thinking about all of the particulars stirred the old man's heartburn, but it had to be done.

"Alright, Detective. You are a thirteen-year-old boy from the Seventeenth with no daddy who loves Louis Armstrong and trumpet and can't talk. What are you doing right now?" Melancon asked, looking down at the black surface of his coffee.

Felix was quiet for a long time.

"You're a lot closer to thirteen than me, Felix, you'll have to help me out."

"To be honest with you..." Felix hesitated. Melancon turned to face him.

"I'm distracted."

"Distracted by what?"

"By the thought of what happens to the kid next when we *do* find him. I mean, what would happen to him if he walked right through our front door, at this very moment, and sat down on the couch?"

"Well...we'd have to take him to the police, Felix. He's a witness in a homicide investigation. The only witness, maybe."

"And after that?"

Melancon quietly sipped his coffee, turned his back again.

"Well," Felix started, "here's the way I look at it. He probably hasn't been reported as missing yet to the police...at least not by that uncle. It would just make him look bad, right? So, I don't think it's our job to report him missing to the police, either. That's up to his family. And reporting him missing to the police doesn't necessarily do him any favors. On the other hand, he probably knows enough to go to the police if he's in fear for his life, even though he also knows he'll have to talk. And he clearly does not want to talk. Or to be with his uncle. Otherwise, they're just going to stick him in some home, aren't they? That's where all this is headed, unless the stepmama recovers real quick."

Melancon, for once, held his tongue.

"I'd probably rather be free myself," Felix went on. "And I'd probably go to whatever lengths I had to to make sure I was free. I've heard Tina talk about those homes, the ones they put wayward children in, and yeah, I believe I'd rather take my chances on the street."

"He's a thirteen-year-old boy," Melancon said.

"Exactly. He's young, but not too young to make his own decisions about some things."

"We made a promise to an old friend, Felix. One who we owe a huge debt to, and one who also happens to take promises very seriously. At least if we find Andre, we know he's safe. We can tell Tomás he is safe. We owe him that much. Problem is we've got no leads. And no suspect for his father's murder. Now, what does that mean?"

"Means the killer is still out there. It means that if the killer knows Andre is the only witness, he's probably looking for the kid too."

"And so, this isn't just about going to an orphanage, Felix. This could be life or death. Fact is, we've got jack shit to go on, and we had better get busy being detectives."

Felix shook his head. He reached into his pocket and placed Andre's cell phone down on the desk between himself and his partner.

"We've got *this*," the young man said.

Melancon sat down at the desk and peered down at the little black phone. It was a bit out of date. Smaller. Not the big glassy mirror he saw most kids carrying these days.

"You look through it?" he asked Felix.

"The numbers all look like they were put in by an adult. Just by the way they're written. Mr. Julian Oliver – Music Teacher. Sarah Weinberger – Child Psychologist. Uncle Melph. Mother. Father."

Felix's lower lip seemed to quiver a bit on the last entry. He sat across from Melancon, and they both stared down at the device together.

"I'll call the music teacher," Melancon said suddenly and snatched the thing up before Felix could object.

"Yes, is this Julian Oliver?"

Melancon gave the thumbs-up, pointed at the notepad on the desk.

"Yes, this is Detective David Melancon. I'm calling in regard to a certain student of yours....Yes....No, he is...well hopefully alright....Andre Adai....Okay, would it be possible for my partner and me to stop by your office this morning? We just need to ask you a few questions....Thank you.... Okay. Eight works for you?... Okay. Right there on St. Charles?...Okay."

Melancon slapped the phone shut.

"Let's go," he said.

The fineness of the spring morning was fully apparent, even to their heavy eyes, as the detectives bumped and jostled down the Avenue. The air was crisp and flower-smelling, petals and pollen swirling on the root-broke sidewalk, the wispy clouds already melting from a cobalt sky. The crepe myrtles along the sidewalk were in glorious bloom, still bedecked with beads from the many parades.

Melancon stopped at a gas station and had Felix pump some air into his sagging front tire while he checked the dipstick's shade.

Julian Oliver's house was another Victorian, not nearly as grand as the Herbert family home, but stately nonetheless. It looked to be just another residence, unless your eyes happened to alight on a small plaque out by the gate that read "Julian Oliver – Music Instructor." It listed no phone number or contact information. That, combined with the St. Charles address, told Melancon that either this was a side gig or the man must be one of the most inexplicably successful music teachers this side of the Mississippi.

They found him on his side porch, clean-shaven with a few large birthmarks on his left cheek, which was ruddy in the morning air. His hair was prematurely graying and thinning, and he kept it plastered back on his head.

"Julian Oliver," he said, taking no great pains to hide the suspicious study he made of both detectives. "What do you want?"

Melancon raised his hands in mock submission. "You could relax a bit, first of all. We aren't here to arrest you or anything."

The man narrowed his eyes at Melancon, his head

bobbing slightly and his cheeks growing even redder than before.

"Why don't you tell me what's happened, and I'll decide whether or not to relax."

Julian had a faint accent that Melancon was only just able to peg as British. Not the refined, posh English of the upper-class Londoner, though. Something else. Maybe even a little Scottish thrown into the mix. It seemed it had been Americanized over a long period but lingered at the edges.

"Where you from?" Melancon tried.

Julian didn't answer but continued staring at the two of them with deepening lines spreading across his forehead.

"Look, we're friends. We're here because Andre Adai's father was killed."

Julian's shoulders tensed, but the sharp angles of his brow released into concerned curves. He sat down quietly on one of his wicker porch chairs and motioned for the detectives to do the same.

"I'm sorry," he said.

Melancon waited. Neither detective sat down. Their eyes drifted over to connect with each other for the briefest of conferences.

Julian waved his hands around the porch apologetically, as if they were all huddled in a shanty rather than on the porch of a mansion. "I'm a bachelor, so I'm afraid I can't really offer you proper tea and biscuits."

"That's fine," Melancon said, finally sitting down, still carefully studying the man. Felix sat as well, squinting in the early-morning light and trying that disarming smile of his.

"You must understand. People talk when you're an unmarried man who privately tutors kids. One rumor gets started and...well, I don't have to tell you chaps. When I get a call from private detectives, in this environment, I become a bit panicked."

Melancon chose to let the silence, long and stretched out and awkward, linger until it became a bit painful.

Julian shook his head. "But, I'm...Andre. I can't believe such a thing has happened. You say his father was killed? Can you say what happened?"

"Not exactly. The crime is still fresh, under investigation."

"Oh my God. So, he was murdered? You haven't caught the...the perpetrator yet?"

They watched him.

Julian's hazel eyes went from one detective to another with increasing speed. "You aren't saying?"

"Certainly not," Felix broke in, lifting the tension at once with a smile and a friendly lilt to his voice. "We aren't actually investigating the murder. At least, not officially. We're just trying to fill in some missing pieces here. You haven't heard from Andre, by any chance?"

Melancon was impressed with his young partner. Felix was learning how to take all of the subtle, unanswerable tension right to the edge. To use it, harnessing awkwardness to compel speech. And also how to cut the tension right before you lost a potential source of information, just at the right moment, so they would open up the floodgates and be on your side throughout the casual interrogation that followed.

But Julian seemed to have been oddly stunned by it all and remained far from a gushing font of conversation. He slowly shook his head, apparently considering his timeline carefully. His mouth hung open and his eyes traced a passing streetcar out on the Avenue.

"No, no. Our last lesson would have been a few days ago. Maybe Tuesday? I can check my—"

"That won't be necessary," Melancon said. "We're here just to try and learn a little bit more about Andre. As you probably know, the kid keeps his cards sort of close to his chest."

Melancon looked for that smile of recognition and understanding from Julian, a friendly mutual reckoning about a young pupil, but the teacher remained dazed.

"I'm sorry, I'm just trying to process all this," he finally said.

"We understand Andre is interested in music," Felix went on, "which must have made you two close.

We were hoping you could elaborate a little on...just what kind of a boy Andre is."

"Oh my," Julian said, a crushed look settling on his features. "I think you had better come inside."

The detectives found a very clean and well-ordered studio downstairs, an assortment of instruments that neither of them could have named. Some were exotic and mysterious; others were of that shining brass quality that one saw nearly every day on the streets downtown. They all had their places—their hooks and stands and corners. Sheets of music lined the front of a grand piano, jet black. In one corner an old Wurlitzer jukebox caught Melancon's appreciative eye. It looked well polished and held the light of the early morning, now streaming in beautifully through the large windows.

"Nice place," Melancon said, looking at Mr. Oliver with as much suggestion as he could muster.

"I have some pictures I'd like to show you," Julian said and gestured the detectives over to a far wall.

The first was a framed photograph of a tow-headed boy, his mouth agape in silent song. He stood in front of a music stand, with wires and microphones surrounding him in the background.

"Nephew of yours?" Felix guessed.

A slight smile played on Julian's lips—tight, tired, perhaps a bit condescending. "That, gentlemen, is a young man named Aksel Rykkvin, of Norway. This is him midperformance with the Oslo Philharmonic, during which the king and queen were both in attendance. The king is said to have come to tears over the beauty of the child's voice. You see, Aksel is a vocalist, a soprano at the moment, though that will surely change. But he has one of the most astonishing voices the world has ever heard."

The two detectives politely leaned in, each in turn, and studied the photograph.

"He is thirteen," Julian said and waved them on to the next picture on the wall.

In the next photograph, a young, chubby-faced Asian girl in a flowing dress cradled a violin beneath her chin. She stood on a bright wooden stage with a large piano in the background.

"Lee Soo-Bin," Julian continued. "She has a tone so perfect that it would make you weep. Flawless technique. She is but sixteen now but is destined to become one of the foremost concert violinists in the world."

"And here."

He moved past them to the next photo, in which a young child was cradling a ukulele in his lap, sitting on the lip of a fountain and staring at a pigeon that had landed nearby.

"Feng E, a slightly less conventional musician. He gained fame on YouTube. Taiwanese, twelve, and absolutely brilliant on any set of strings. He's still quite young but has already become a master in eight different instruments."

Julian now waved to an empty space on the wall.

"And this...barren spot you see here, gentlemen. This is where, one day, I will put Andre Adai."

Felix's eyes widened. Melancon nodded his head.

"You see, chaps, when you ask me if Andre is interested in music, it's like asking if Shakespeare fancied a bit of poetry and prose...or asking if Van Gogh was interested in paint and color and a summer sky...like asking if Einstein liked physics or...well, you get the idea. Andre Adai is but thirteen, and already he's one of the finest trumpet players the world has ever seen. He has a gift that you and I would struggle to comprehend."

"So, he's a prodigy?" Melancon asked.

"Yes," Julian said, straightening his back and heaving his chest out a few additional inches, "I suppose that is the word that one might use."

"What word would you use?" Felix asked.

The music instructor turned his head towards Felix, strode past him and walked over to the far wall, on which were more instruments, pictures, and framed records. He looked them up and down, addressing the detectives over his shoulder.

"That lad is destined for greatness."

"Greatness...," Felix echoed.

"Or perhaps I should say *was* destined for greatness, seeing as how he has suffered an unspeakable tragedy during one of his formative, crucial periods of development. Trauma like that, at such a young age, does not bode well for Andre's future."

Melancon put a hand to his chin. "And so why this blank space on the wall where Andre should go? The other kids are the same age and they're already playing for kings and queens. I suppose Andre hasn't been invited to play Carnegie Hall just yet?"

"That *is* why, in fact. Andre is great to be sure, but his greatness, his potential, has yet to be realized. His endurance, his purity of tone, his soulful musicality so free of ego. Andre is the kind of trumpet player that comes along once a century. His life, if stewarded correctly, is to be a series of accolades, accomplishments, and universal acclaim. He may have started off a poor boy from the Seventeenth Ward, but he would certainly not end up that way given the right guidance. Though, based on what you've told me, I fear it may be too late."

Felix raised an eyebrow. "I'm still not getting it...I mean, what's the holdup? These other kids aren't much older than Andre and they've already been making such big moves. Why hasn't Andre?"

Julian looked down onto the old cypress floor. "It is not for me to decide. Nor to comment on such things, but I suppose you've spoken to Andre's psychologist? She's just down the street, after all."

"No."

"You mean you came here first?"

"Well, like we said," Felix went on, "we knew he liked music. That's about all we know. We thought maybe you could help us find him."

"Find him? I don't follow."

The two detectives looked at one another.

"You mean to tell me that you've lost one of this generation's most promising musical minds?"

"Something like that, yeah," the older detective said. "Any idea where a kid like that might get off to?"

"Detectives, you are aware that Andre does not speak, correct?"

"He didn't speak to us, anyway. Though we have heard he does speak a bit to people he feels comfortable around. We were hoping that maybe you two had that kind of relationship...that maybe he was a bit more comfortable with you."

Julian shook his head sharply. "The boy and I have worked together for over two years now, and he has never spoken a word to me. He is, however, a great student. Highly intelligent and attentive, utterly capable. He has focus, persistence, and an ear like you wouldn't believe. I must say that—"

Just then, Melancon's phone started to ring. He put a finger up to Julian and left Felix to finish the interrogation.

Out on the porch, he answered the call. It was Janine.

"David."

"Hey there. Kind of busy at the—"

"We've got a guy in custody. ID'd him from a camera on the corner of Oak and Carrollton. He was running full sprint away from the crime scene, specks of blood on his shirt. Turns out he has a rap sheet a mile long. We need to bring Andre in to ID him, just for confirmation. Now I'm not asking your permission, I'm just asking for your blessing, we need to—"

"Damnit, Janine."

"Don't curse at me, David. Now I thought you'd be happy to hear about this, but if you aren't going to be a willing participant in this, then—"

"We'll be down there soon. I'll explain later."

He hung up before she could let him have it, and silently wished he had given himself a few more drinking years before drying out.

TEN

Louis Armstrong is thirteen years old and has spent all his young life mostly just needing someone to point him towards a good place. In the Waif's Home for Boys he would find Mr. Peter Davis, who knew the way to the *best* place. Somehow, he knew. The books don't say how it all happened, but I've played it out in my mind so many times it's like a video I can start and stop anytime I want.

Think of it like this.

Little Louis Armstrong is blue. He's sitting by the window in the Waif's Home. Sometimes he has these fat tears quietly rolling down his cheeks, sometimes not. He tries to make sure that no one can see them when they do show up. All of the other boys are studying French, repeating lines from a textbook, but not Louis. He doesn't care about French much, because he doesn't know how one day he will dine in

Paris, how he will someday bring New Orleans to Old Orleans. Right now there is a huge cloud over him, getting bigger and darker, and he just cares about the fact that he is completely alone in the world. Are there bars on the window? Probably not. Can he see the city living outside? He must, at least at a distance.

The one thing he can never see is the future. But that doesn't stop him from painting a picture of it anyway. There are no kings and queens and magazines in the future he sees, though. From where he sits, everything ahead looks dark and gray and hateful. It looks poor and hard and small and maybe not worth carrying on with at all, which is kind of how I feel right now, standing in his park under his statue and hearing that music come drifting down to me, pulling me towards it. But where is it coming from?

Mr. Peter Davis sees the boy crying. He keeps on with the French lesson, for now.

But he knows about Louis. Somehow. He sees that satchel mouth and those blubbering tears. He sees the big, broken heart. He sees his soul, maybe.

And maybe, even, he sees the future.

Because afterwards Mr. Davis calls Louis into his office. Peter is a tall man with wooly hair and a large, bobbing Adam's apple. He's got big, kind eyes just like Louis does and a wind that won't quit, just like little Louis. He's got *musicality*, and so maybe he can spot it in a waif as well. He smiles down at this boy in his office, this boy who looks to be disappearing. Maybe Mr. Peter Davis had something magic about him, because what he did next changed the whole world to be at least ten percent more wonderful than it would have been otherwise.

"Louis," he said. "Louis, look here."

And then Mr. Davis put an old case down on the desk between them, snapped the buckles off, lifted the lid. Where did it come from?

The hinges creaked; Louis peered inside.

Sitting there was the treasure he had been missing his whole life. It wasn't a daddy. It wasn't dirty coins picked up off the street. It wasn't a gun.

It was brass.

It glowed there in that office, maybe, that weapon that would win every fight without a drop of blood. *Maybe* it glowed or maybe it was old and tarnished and pitiful looking, the books just don't say. I think it was somewhere in between.

Airports, stadiums, statues. Louis on a camel in Egypt, blowing for the dead pharaohs. The cameras all zooming in from a thousand angles across all the places he would go, all in Technicolor, right on his sweat-dropping, grand-smiling face. Right into the heart of everything beautiful and happy that comes up from the wet, slimy gutter of this place. For five decades he would give the world unbridled joy from the fat end of the—

"Go ahead, pick it up," Mr. Peter Davis said.

I can't stand it anymore. The music is coming from somewhere. I can't stop myself. I can't find it but I'm desperate to try. I run and run some more. Towards the music, or at least, I hope. I trip over an egg crate, pick myself up and keep running.

"Pick it up, Louis. It's a cornet, you ever seen one before?" Mr. Peter Davis asks.

I run as fast as I can until my wind gives out. A car screeches its tires and honks at me.

Little Louis hoists the cornet, his eyes getting wide and his breath getting still.

"Go on, see if you can blow it, Louis."

I run through the streets, past the shuttered-up buildings. This is all Storyville. A place that is gone and lives only in the past and is now something completely changed. But the music, the sound is still there, and I am headed towards that brass-belching, gold-throated music. It is getting louder, closer, warmer.

When I get there, I find three boys, young men really. They're older than me. When I see them I stop and finally put my hands on my knees and lean forward in my too-large army jacket, gasping for breath. For a second, I imagine that I'm going to vomit, and it's lucky that none of them have looked my way just yet. They're proper teenagers, now that I see them clearly, much older than me, maybe eighteen or nineteen, all jerseys and denim and beanies marching through the streets with big, hard instruments swinging out ahead of them. They have muscles and move with purpose.

The biggest, a stocky boy with orange hair, has a tuba. A skinny one with dreads and a blue jersey has a trombone.

And then I see the big bass drum, carried by a sad-faced kid with a Saints cap. I see the words written on it.

"Big Waif Brass Band," it says.

I wipe my mouth with the sleeve of the jacket, catch my breath as quick as I can, pull out my trumpet. Then I step out in front of them.

They keep playing little ditties, small licks and scales, more tuning and horseplay than anything. They step around me without a second glance and go marching on down the street. I count them. And then I count them again, considering the instrument that each of them carries.

They have no trumpet.

I don't know if there is such a thing as destiny or not, but I run down another block, meet them again. This time I press my horn to my lips but am stopped still by some big invisible grip on my chest.

I don't know what to do. The boys are big and mean looking. I've seen their type before. They keep moving past me, like water moving around a rock in the river. I try to smile at them but I can't. I try to call out for them to stop and see me, but I can't do that either.

The next block, orange-haired Tuba finally asks me, "What you want, kid?"

I press the horn to my lips, imagine I am standing somewhere I'm not really standing. A place far away. I'm in Storyville and it's 100 years ago. Before all these lights and cement and overpasses. But also, I'm in a place that hasn't even happened yet, so far ahead that it can't be seen. When I get to where I'm going, my lungs fill with air on their own, my lips purse just right on the mouthpiece without even trying, and I let out one long, pure note. The high C.

Tuba cocks his head. Framed by that great circle of metal, with the orange hair, it looks almost like an old painted portrait. Trombone nods and Bass Drum slams a few deep thunder rolls.

"What's your name, kid?" Tuba asks me.

I shake my head at him.

"Your folks not around?" he asks, looking behind me.

I shake my head at him.

"What you doing out here?"

I shake my head again and play him a flurry of notes, a rainstorm of sound twisting up in a great crescendo. I put my whole chest into it and near split my lip. The echo of it goes down the long street and bounces off the hurricane shutters and front porches and oak trees.

The Big Waif Brass Band gets real quiet. Trombone stops making its little runs. Bass Drum's arms hang down long at his side.

"Where you learn that?" Tuba asks.

I shake my head.

They lean into each other, talking in low voices, casting glances back at me.

"How old are you, boy?"

I shake my head.

They talk more, making little sideways glances in my direction. I put my horn back up to my lips and am about to blow again when they turn back around, all as one.

"You want to make some money, kid?"

I nod my head.

The young men go back to ignoring me, walking now in a more serious way, like something had sucked the music right out of them for the moment. But Tuba waves his arms for me to follow and keep up. We lug our instruments right down to Esplanade, where we turn towards the river. There are more people on the streets now, some of them wild-eyed, some of them dressed in black with tattoos covering their faces. None of the teenagers ask me any more questions or try to talk to me again, which I am very glad for. They talk amongst each other, though—about girls and a fight they saw the night before.

We walk on the neutral ground, past circles of cardboard with shirtless men squatting in the center of them. These men are dirty, hairy. Their faces are thin, and some of them look up at me with pure disgust and anger. One has a bone going right through his nose and he snarls and growls at me just like a dog would.

I'm glad I have the gun. I'm glad I've fallen in with these rough teenagers, too. I know that I might never feel really safe again in my life and I try and tell myself it will be okay. My heart is getting real loud in my chest and I'm wondering if my choices have been the right or wrong ones.

We get down to Frenchman Street, which I've only laid eyes on in the daytime up until now. Now, at night, something has changed about it, something in the air. An energy, all charged up and neon.

We come down to a particular corner and stop. The big teenagers are shaking hands with other big teenagers, and I try to keep mostly out of sight behind Tuba. There's a blue wall behind us that belongs to a building that's all boarded up and dark. There are clubs up and down the block, bright blue and pink and green light falling out of their doors. I smell beer and hear distant music, but this spot where we're stopped is mostly quiet, mostly abandoned.

People who are passing on the street start to notice

us. Their necks crane and some of them slow down. Bass Drum lets out a few big strikes, and I remember that I don't know where I'm going to sleep tonight.

A couple of the same shirtless young men pass by, their cheeks full of metal. One of them has a big pit bull on a chain walking in front of them, and the dog stops too and turns to look at me. His girlfriend is lanky and has a dirty shirt on that says "Love Not Hate." There are also men with nice suits and women with nice dresses. Some of them are coming towards us now, forming a semicircle out in the street so that the cars have to pass real slow and honk their horns. I wonder what is going to happen, because the air is getting tighter and tighter somehow.

Finally, Tuba announces in a big voice that we'll start in five minutes. Another teenager appears with a box and a handful of CDs. Another appears with a red wagon, and in the wagon is an ice chest. They all shake hands with each other, but no one tries to shake with me, and for that I'm glad.

"COLD BEER," the wagon man shouts, scaring me with the suddenness of his voice.

"COLD BEER, ONE DOLLAR."

His wagon has a squeaky wheel and he's smoking weed. I can smell it settling over everything, funky and strong. I realize that it smells just like Uncle Melph's jacket that I'm wearing. The crowd begins to crush in tighter and tighter. Some of them have red faces, some of them are kissing at each other, and some just look at me blankly. Now none of the cars on the street can pass, and the honking gets loud and constant but none of the people seem to pay any mind to the traffic.

Now our band has grown. Two more musicians: a saxophone and a snare drum. Maybe they came out of the darkened alley behind us, or maybe they were there all along, growing out of the sidewalk like weeds. They announced themselves loudly with their instruments.

And then the whole Big Waif Brass Band quiets down for a second, looking at one another, nodding, looking at me. They swing their long teenager arms, and Snare Drum runs a comb through his hair. The crowd is getting crazier with every lick or trill or drum-roll: pressing in on us, pressing in on the street, grabbing beer cans from the wagon man, screaming and hollering and dancing and arguing. Somewhere I hear a siren go off, but it doesn't matter. There is nowhere else to go now. I am trapped in here by the crowd, we all are. I shudder, thinking how I can't leave, but then my heart slows down finally because now I know it's not a choice I have to make. It has been made for me. The wagon man passes me and presses a can into my hands, and now my hands are wet and cold. The smell of beer makes me queasy, and Daddy always told me not to grow up and become a drinker, but I nod at the wagon man anyway, putting the can down at my feet where I won't accidentally decide to drink it. I'm already thirsty and I have no water.

Tuba lets out a few deep, shaking growls—more orderly this time, leading up to something. Snare Drum follows, dancing lightly on the skin, then Bass Drum hits so hard that I can feel it in the soles of my shoes. Then Trombone starts to slide and we're going off.

I might never be happy again, I'm afraid. There's no place for me to go after this is all over. But there is relief in the world for sadness and hurt, if even just for a moment. Not even relief, really. Just something that stops you from breaking apart into a million pieces.

The brass cries out around me and I can stand here with the same sadness and pain in my chest, but for just a split second it's okay to hurt such a way. The pain almost feels good, like when you scratch poison ivy, even though you shouldn't, and it hurts worse later because you did.

My fingers and lips start to itch, just like that.

I'm thinking too much, until I notice that the whole band is looking at me in that way that people do when they're expecting something out of you. I know it's time for me to stop thinking. Bass Drum nods at me almost angrily, and Tuba's bug eyes have me a little scared the way they press down into me.

I've got to earn my right to stand here, and I know it.

I bring the trumpet to my lips, try to think if I've ever been here before. I mean, playing for so many people. I'm a shy person, I guess. I almost have a panic attack, right there on Frenchman Street. But then I start thinking about Louis Armstrong and—

I press the mouthpiece into my mouth and blow.

I keep blowing it until what is in the future and what is in the past have gone completely away from me. Even Louis is gone. I don't know what is going to happen, and I don't care. All of the pictures in my head fade.

When I open my eyes again, everyone on the street is staring at me. Happy faces, red with the beer and whiskey and music, just beam at me from out of the crowd. Some of them clap, and the cardboard box that is sitting in front of the Big Waif Brass Band starts to fill up real quick.

The band members are looking at me too. They don't smile but I can tell they're waiting on me. They want me to lead the next one.

So, I do. I start the next song. It's probably cheesy to them, lame, an old piece of history. But it will always be one of my favorites. I choose it because suddenly I feel powerful, unafraid. I have always wanted to stand out on the street and play it loud just like the men in Jackson Square do. And now I am.

I started it off that way, with the long, happy, bright licks of the trumpet. It's a song about the end of the world, Mr. Julian told me that. But to hear it, you would think that the end of the world is the most beautiful thing that could ever be. And maybe it is.

To my surprise, Tuba starts to sing. He has a deep, baritone voice that's just like his instrument, but perfectly full of soul and he can even hit the high notes just right.

Oh when the saints...

I open my eyes between two great big licks.

go marching in...

I feel my feet start to move. I'm dancing.

Oh when the saints go marching in...

I twist around and blow the horn, and suddenly I'm happy. Just for that moment.

But it doesn't last long. Not even ten seconds. I shouldn't have opened my eyes, just that bit too soon. I shouldn't even be here, trapped as I am. The perfect came and went and now I see a face in the crowd. The face is masked, with a sequined type of eye cover that you see usually see at Mardi Gras—the same kind of glitzy things that hang on the walls of the tourist traps on Bourbon.

Yes, I want to be in that number.

The face is wearing a mask, but I know it. Where I know it from, or who it is behind those sequins, I'm sure I couldn't say. What is sure is that it is getting closer, moving quickly through the crowd. The body it is attached to is not dancing, not making merry, not twisting and shaking with the music, which makes it stand out from the crowd of happy, jostling drinkers. I can't be sure—the nose, the area around the eyes, the brow. Who can know their shape behind that mask? But I can see the mouth, and the shade of it gives me this sick feeling in my stomach.

The face is coming towards me.

Oh when the sun, refused to shine.

It's not smiling, but pushing and shoving and coming, pointing directly at me. My insides freeze up for a second and the sound of my horn begins to falter.

Oh when the trumpet, it sounds its call.

Coming quicker now, pushing right through the crowd, parting them like Moses.

I blow a flat note. The fear is too much now. In another second the dark figure will be upon me. The band are looking at me but they keep right on playing and singing.

I look down into the cardboard box at my feet. There are many one-dollar bills, but a handful of twenties as well.

There are only a few bodies now between me and the dark figure.

I reach down into the box of folding money, take the biggest scoop of it I can.

A hand grabs me from out of the crowd. The masked face looms over me now.

I crumple the bills in my fist, into a little ball as

tight and small as I am able, and then I shove the bills into my mouth and yank my body back out of the grip of the hand. I fall on my back and I'm too terrified to even look up. From down there, through a forest of legs and hips moving, I see a hole, a way out, and I plunge into it headlong.

I'm hitting knees and dodging sneakers, I'm weaving and ducking, I'm nearly crushed. I keep my horn pointed out in front of me like the cowcatcher on a train, and then I'm out again, out into the street.

The money in my mouth tastes dry and cottony with just a slight tang to it. I use my tongue to tuck it back into my cheek and I run.

I'm running down the neutral ground of Esplanade as fast as I can, the iron balconies and bent oaks and headlights all a blur. I've got my horn held tight in my left hand, swinging the weight of it to make myself faster. I can feel the gun in my backpack bouncing against my lower back. When I start to run short on breath, I take the money out of my mouth, try to flatten it against my leg, and then stuff it in my pocket, looking behind myself to make sure I don't see that face following me in the night. I don't, and I get down past the houses and all until I come to an area with some small hotels. I know it's a bad idea, but I'm scared and cold and hungry, so I duck into the one with the most light coming from the lobby.

The man behind the counter is dark and has thick

eyebrows, and I get the feeling that nothing surprises him. Those eyebrows don't even begin to jump or react, even me running in with my horn, out of breath and not saying a word. He just looks at me like he has seen such a thing a hundred times.

I put down a few of the crumpled, slightly wet bills of the counter and look at him. He looks down at the money and then back up at me.

"ID?" he says.

I fumble around in my pockets until I come to that sad piece of plastic. Maybe I shouldn't, but I do, because ethical dilemmas don't mean much when you're cold and hungry and maybe being hunted by someone who wants to do you harm. I hand him Daddy's RTA badge and try to set my face just right.

He looks at it, then looks at me.

"Renato?"

I nod my head.

"How's the streetcar line doing these days?"

I nod my head.

The guy cracks a smile and slaps the ID back on the counter, but he doesn't push it towards me.

"So, you want to wait over there while I call the cops?"

I shake my head, point at the plastic badge again. When he doesn't move, I go to pick it up, but he snatches it away from me and cracks that terrible smirk once again.

"Possession of stolen identification is a crime, young man. Who is this, your daddy? Where is he?"

I get upset.

"What do you got, a girlfriend or something? Why don't you kids just do it in the park or the back of a car or something? Not at my hotel."

The man waves his arms in front of him, back and forth. I lunge again for my daddy's ID badge, which as a poor waif, I know is going to be the only real thing I have of him except what's locked away inside my own mind.

But the clerk is quicker than me, and he tucks the badge into his shirt pocket and makes a tutting sound at me. I stare death at him, but it's obvious that it's going to take more than a look for this man to give an inch.

"What, what are you going to do?" he says.

I stare.

"Go on, kid, I have real problems to deal with. I'll give the badge to the cops and they'll contact Renato, nothing to worry about. Got to make sure the people who make this city run are taken care of, after all. What's a streetcar driver going to do without his ID badge, kid? What are you thinking?"

I stare, so angry that I feel like the gun in my backpack has started to glow hot, burning my back. But I'm not angry at him, I remind myself. I have to remind myself of that three times. The badge is just a piece of plastic, that's all it is, really. This man doesn't know anything about who I am or who my daddy was or what happened to him.

But on my way out, I see a lamp sitting on a table just begging to be pushed off. It is pleading with me to shatter it. I stare at it for a second, trying to wrestle with all the anger I feel. The man calls out to me but I'm off and running again, before I let the anger take over, afterwards realizing that I left the money sitting there on the asshole's counter.

I'm not very good at being a waif, I decide.

I head up under the I-10 bridge, because I know that this is where a person goes to sleep if they have no home, like me. The dusty, grassless ground beneath the bridge used to be a big avenue where a lot of Mardi Gras parades happened, but now it's nothing but a dark cave filled with pigeons and tents and doo-doo and all sorts of bottles and cans. Some sad person painted big oak trees on the concrete pillars, maybe so that they could try to remember the big street that had once been there with leaf shade overhead instead of a bridge. There are Carnival Indians painted on some, long brass instruments painted on another. But all of this color looks washed out in the streetlamps, and without grass and shops and a streetcar this is not a happy place. As I walk further, the number of tents grows until it's nothing but a sea of them, a whole camp of tents waving and blowing in the breeze. I shudder, looking at the little town within a town. I don't have any tent, so instead I crawl up into a little hole in the dirt up against a concrete platform.

You couldn't call it sleeping, what I do there huddled in the dirt. I'm too cold, and too scared to do anything but shut my eyes for about thirty seconds at a time. At about three in the morning, it gets even worse. If you've ever put your head to the ground and heard the sound of the big thoroughbreds that the policemen and women ride around town, coming up into your skull, then you know why homeless people look so bad in the morning. When I hear that sound (clop, clop, clop) coming through at about three in the morning, I know that my running isn't done for the day.

Because even though Louis Armstrong became what he would become in the Waif's Home, I'm not ready yet to do that. It seems to me that being put away somewhere might be worse than being cold and shivering up under a bridge.

Two of them, a man and a woman, come in their dark blue uniforms. They ride kind of slow but you can see their belts and badges and guns all glowing underneath those streetlamps. They get down when they see a man lying on his back between two tents. The male officer pokes him with a long stick. The sleeper rolls over and lets out a loud moan, and the officers let him be.

I start to slide out of my hiding spot, slow and quiet

like, and get my backpack all ready and tight. But I'm stiff from laying on the cold ground, and one of my legs doesn't act like I want it to. I trip up and fall, and when I do, the lady officer points right at me.

"Hey, kid!" she calls out and puts her hand on either her radio or her gun. I don't wait around to see which one. Instead I take off running at full speed out into the neighborhood. I hop a fence and jog through a parking lot, then another one, the whole time listening for the horrible *clop clop* sound behind me.

At the third fence, my backpack gets caught on a barb. Since my horn, at the fat end, is just a little too big for my backpack, and I can't zip it up all the way, my horn falls out onto the pavement, making a huge metal sound. For a minute I'm sure I'm fixing to be shipped off to the Waif's Home and almost make up my mind to give up, because I'm getting so tired of running. But no one comes. I wait, at least less cold after my run. Then I scoop up my horn and carry it in my hand until I come over to Tulane Avenue.

I stare for about five minutes at the big new hospital they built there, all glass and lit up. It doesn't match anything around here, and I wonder if that was the point of the whole thing. A lot of the houses and things that used to be there are now gone, except for one. There's this big house, painted a hundred different colors and sitting all alone, that seems like it escaped from the bulldozers. The windows and door are all blocked up with plywood, but it stands up off the ground on a couple of cinder blocks, which is just like our shotgun back in the Seventeenth. That's how I know what to do, even though it's not a plan I particularly like all that much.

I try not to think about spiders, about rats, about snakes and all of the other creepy crawlers that had the same notion as me as I slide up under the house. I try to think about Louis Armstrong instead. It's warmer up under the house. There is no cement, no wind, and no horse sounds, so I press myself up against the dirt and pull the army jacket real tight against me.

I pull it tighter and tighter until I feel—

There's something in the pocket of the old army jacket—something hard and solid that I hadn't felt there before. I run my hands up and down it on the outside of the coat. There are so many pockets, it takes me a moment before I find the small zipper on the inside and—

Bullet shells.

I know what bullet shells are from so long ago that I'm not sure if the memory is real or not. I remember sitting in a wooden box way up in the middle of the woods. I'm sitting with my daddy and with—

Bullet shells, in the jacket. Something tells me not to touch them too much, so after I make sure what they are, I carefully zip the little pocket back up and lay there in the dark, shivering and wondering why this jacket would have bullet shells in it. But I'm too tired, hungry, cold and afraid to do any real figuring.

So, I let it go. I think about Louis instead. I play through his life in my mind, over and over again, until I forget where I am. I forget about the cold, the spiders, the rats.

Louis Armstrong is fourteen years old. He stands on Rampart Street, which is not far from this old house I'm up under. This was before the overpass, before the hospital, before everything got torn down and flooded and bulldozed and shut down for vice. Behind Louis is a long line of waifs. All of them are in tattered rags, some of their shirts are made from cornmeal bags and others from old faded curtains. They are hungry but not starving. Cold but not freezing. They sleep with a roof over their heads and have three small meals every day guaranteed thanks to Mr. Peter Davis.

Mr. Peter Davis, long and lanky and dressed in a scuffed old suit himself, is standing at the back of the procession. He has a top hat in his hand and is smiling. The residents of both the Quarter and Tremé are standing out in the street, watching the boys who are watching them back.

"Good morning, ladies and gentlemen," Mr. Peter Davis cries out to the crowd. His voice is loud and clear and carries with it all the soul of New Orleans. He calls out over the clomping hooves of horses (clop, clop) and the chatter of the mamas and sisters and aunties who are out tossing their pots into the street or flapping long white pieces of laundry, beating rugs and all the other sounds of life.

"My name is Mr. Peter Davis, and I'm the head of musical instruction for the Colored Waif's Home for Boys. Today, I'm very proud to announce that the boys have marched down this morning in order to play for you. Any and all donations will be much appreciated and will go towards new uniforms for our boys."

Some of the men watching laugh. Comments are made about the raggedy state of the boys—some words colorful and fun, and some not so.

"Alright now, Louis. Do your thing, boy," Mr. Pete whispers and nods his head like a proud father might do.

Louis smiles that smile. The one he will use for the rest of his life to put skeptics at ease, to worm his way down into your heart before he has even started to blow. He smiles and beams at the crowd. The cornet goes to his lips, the snare begins to pitter-patter, the bugle to wail, the sound of this place that comes up from the swampy ground in a way that no one can resist no matter how hard they try.

And then Louis lets out the first note. It's slow at first but rises and twists. It throws all of the other instruments into the background.

The laundry sounds stop. The gossipers lose

interest in their gossip and the men don't dare to crack another joke.

The waifs march all through the neighborhood, smiling, blowing, beating, bowing, dancing, working and making everyone that sees them fall in love. Pocketbooks come out, coin purses, billfolds. This time the money goes into the top hat instead of cast out on the street. Every coin that goes in, every shining piece of silver, allows Louis's smile to grow a little wider, for his back to straighten just a little bit more, and for his horn to blow in a way that is a little less tired and scared and alone.

But in the crowd, there is a dark face.

It doesn't smile but gets bigger, meaner closer.

It gets so close that I can finally make its features out, features that a boy can never forget.

When I see that face, I wake up under the darkness of that old house, and even though I'm freezing cold, my body is wet with sweat.

ELEVEN

It was indeed only a short walk from the music teacher's studio to Dr. Sarah Weinberger's clinic. Melancon had the opportunity to wonder, on his bright stroll through the uptown sunshine, why it was that psych clinics were never to be found in poor neighborhoods—in those places where the people might have real, honest-to-God problems to contend with. Instead, shrinks were mostly found right here, in the wealthy district, designed around self-indulgent, moneyed whiners. What could make your problems seem more trivial than arriving to your appointment in a hundred-thousand-dollar automobile?

Maybe the lack of sleep was just catching up with him. Not all that was trivial was worthy of scorn. He reminded himself of that fact while admiring the new flowers in bloom, and the way their pollen was causing Felix no end of watery eyes, sneezing, and red skin.

Melancon lit a clove cigarette and looked up at the wavering blossoms with a smile on his weathered face.

"You reckon Julian is clean?" he asked his young, sneezing partner.

Felix cocked his head a bit and wiped at his nose with a handkerchief. "I don't know, the charming Brit is always the bad guy in the movies, right?" he said between sniffles.

"If this was a movie I'd walk out and ask for my money back, probably go bowling instead."

The young man was quiet for a moment.

"He didn't strike me as capable of...you know. But I could see maestro being frustrated with the father, assuming the father didn't play ball with all of Julian's hopes and aspirations for Andre. To hear the way he talked, you could see he had some dreams pinned on the boy. That could make for a tense relationship with the family, especially if the father wanted to keep his son out of the limelight for a while."

Melancon nodded. "Can't say I blame the dad for that. Anyway, seems like we're on the same page. Music teacher strikes me as gentle and honest, if a bit hoity-toity. I was thinking a lot of people have their hopes pinned on Andre. Makes the situation complicated. Let's see what the shrink says about it. In and out, partner. You know I hate these types of places."

"Don't worry, old man, I'm sure she won't throw any diagnosis your way. Not for free, anyhow. I've got a few guesses, though; you can have them pro bono if you want."

"That won't be necessary, Felix."

Dr. Sarah Weinberger, PsyD, as her sign read, did not have a secretary. But the two detectives happened to catch her just as a tall man with an expensive-looking wristwatch was leaving through her waiting room. Sarah looked at them wide-eyed and uncertain: a middle-aged woman with dirty-blond hair, the faint beginnings of wrinkles, and pale, heavy blue eyes that were becoming crow-footed from, Melancon guessed, a lot of pseudoperceptive squinting.

That was what she was doing now, anyway, as she regarded these two strange men standing before her. Melancon felt himself shudder a bit under the weight of those eyes but tried his best to smile and look nonthreatening as he asked for a moment of her time.

She was prettier up close, had a few freckles that had now all but faded and a bit of a limp as she turned and led them into a well-furnished office without so much as a smile. The walls were plastered with all manner of degrees, certificates, accolades. Melancon took the time, as he often found useful with educated types, to pause and feign interest in these expensive slips of paper. But she didn't seem to notice. The doctor sat in a plush chair in the center of the room and did not invite them to sit on the couch opposite.

"Well?" Her expectant stare tightened the room.

"Sorry to barge in like this, Doctor," he started, a little taken aback by her cool manner. "I'm David Melancon and this is my partner, Felix Herbert. We're private detectives with the Basin Street Detective Agency." Here he flashed her his ID card, flipping out his old buffalo skin wallet.

"I'd like to see that, please," the woman said, after Melancon had already stuffed it back into his coat pocket. She had a lovely, calm voice and a slow way of moving. *Something about shrinks*, Melancon thought to himself. He knew they only pretended to be so in control, but he always felt a slight aversion to a person who betrayed so little. Maybe it was the detective in him, maybe the old card player, or maybe it was just the human being.

She studied the credentials, and then the small badge Melancon sometimes carried to try to put the screws on people.

"I seem to recall that PIs don't carry a badge," the Dr. said in her quiet way.

"Well, it *is* frowned upon."

She nodded and let out a disappointed hum, still fingering the credentials.

Some blood was working its way into Melancon's cheeks now.

"Look, I don't have any legal power over you, miss—"

"Doctor, if you please, and yes, I'm aware of that."

Felix cut in. "We're here about Andre Adai."

"Yes?"

"I wonder if you know that Andre Adai's father has just been killed, and that the boy, who we've come to understand is a patient of yours, has now disappeared."

Her face did not change, except to perhaps lose a touch of color. She relaxed her grip on the credentials just a bit before handing them back over.

"You'll have to share the couch." She pointed.

The two detectives shifted a few magazines and placed themselves down awkwardly, now face-to-face with the shrink in all her placid intensity. Melancon checked her eyes for some sign or meaning, but when she returned his studious gaze, he couldn't help but look away.

"*Has been killed*," she said, almost as if she were speaking to herself. A hand went to her chin. She bit her lip, eyes finding an empty spot on the wall.

"Yes," Felix continued, "he was...um...he was found shot dead while on duty operating the St. Charles streetcar."

"When was this?"

"Monday afternoon."

"Andre was on the streetcar, wasn't he? I know he takes it back home after our appointments."

"Yes, ma'am...yes, Doctor."

Her face finally moved, and when it did it cringed

so that Melancon thought it might crack. She shook her head, rubbing her temples with vigor. The old detective felt himself relax, watching her human emotions finally break through.

"This is a disaster," she said.

The two detectives regarded her quietly.

"That poor boy will never recover from such trauma."

"Well, maybe you can help him with that," Melancon said, regaining his composure. "But we have to find him first."

She cocked her head. "Yes, well, I doubt I'd be able to assist in that."

"Does Andre ever speak to you?" Felix asked from his side of the couch.

"You don't know the details of his condition?"

"We weren't sure he even had a condition."

She stood up, walked over to the window and looked out, her face bathed in the glorious spring sunshine pouring in. "I see him for half price, you know...but Andre's father took extra work just to make sure our appointments continued. It troubled him greatly that Andre didn't go to school, and he wanted to make sure he was looked after by someone qualified in these matters."

They waited.

"You're wondering what *these matters* could possibly mean. It was thought, when Andre was younger, that he might have a mild form of autism. However, as he grew older, it became apparent that this was not the case. Andre seems very comfortable with all nonverbal forms of communication. He is able to maintain eye contact, for instance. He uses hand gestures appropriately. He smiles when he is happy and understands that a smile on someone else means they are happy as well, and so forth. Nothing there consistent with the autism spectrum."

The doctor returned to her penetrating silence for a moment before Felix prodded her on.

"So, what does he have?"

"Andre exhibits classic signs of what we in the community have come to call *selective mutism*. That is, he can talk, he just...chooses not to in almost any situation where he feels the slightest sense of misgiving or anxiety."

Melancon frowned, glancing again at some of the prestigious titles framed on the wall. "So, he's just quiet. That's it?"

She nodded. "You can put it that way if you like."

"And you need all these," he said, gesturing at the diplomas, "to figure that out?"

Felix raised a hand to his partner, who got the picture and leaned back a bit.

"Doctor, are you telling us that Andre doesn't have *any* serious mental issues?"

"No, I'm definitely not telling you that. We *all* have

our issues, Detective," she replied, looking at Melancon suggestively with those pale blue eyes. "Andre is one of the most highly intelligent children I've ever seen. On written IQ exams, he scores in the top ninety-ninth percentile. However, intelligence itself comes with its own set of challenges, now doesn't it?"

"I wouldn't know," Felix said with a smile, causing Melancon to nearly roll his eyes.

"The boy is highly, highly obsessive. He fixates on certain things, like some intelligent people will."

"Such as?"

"Well, he has an obsession with the trumpet, for one. He often practices until his lips burst and bleed. He plays sometimes in the middle of the night, waking up everyone on his block. He takes the instrument with him everywhere he goes, holding it in his arms even during our sessions."

"None of that is normal, then, we can at least agree on that?" Melancon asked.

"Normal...," she echoed.

"Isn't normal your business, Doctor?"

She ignored him, turning her attention back to Felix.

"It's one of the reasons he plays so well. Have you heard Andre play, young man?"

"No, has he played for you?"

"Oh yes, many times."

"So, he is obsessed with his trumpet. Anything else?"

She frowned. "Yes, he also has a severe fixation on Louis Armstrong."

Melancon raised an eyebrow. "But how do you know that, if he doesn't speak to you? Maybe he just likes the music."

"I've had Andre keep journals since he began working with me, almost two years ago. He is a very talented writer, in fact...observant. Observant in a way that most children his age, and even most adults, may not be. He is incredibly sensitive. He just happened to read a biography of Louis Armstrong one day and, well...he has since read nearly everything written on the trumpeter. In fact, Andre's journals are full of references to Armstrong, to the point where...let's just say that I've had some concern about the obsessive nature of Andre's thought process surrounding Armstrong. It's my belief that the boy uses Armstrong to deflect unpleasant sensations and memories, and it has gotten worse since we started our sessions. I sometimes think Andre may even see Armstrong, a sort of imaginary friend, in times of extreme stress. It's fascinating really, the way he has been able to create for himself this *incredible* coping mechanism...based entirely on a man who died thirty-five years before he was ever born. Remarkable. This usually happens only when a child has had some sort of severe trauma in the past."

They waited, Melancon now performing some suggestive glances of his own.

"If you are asking me if Andre has been abused in his past, gentlemen, I can assure you that even I do not know the answer to that. He has never mentioned anything in his journals, nor did his father, who I believe to be...to have been...a thoroughly decent man and as warm and loving as fathers come."

"Where did you last leave it with the boy, Doctor?" Felix asked, leaning in.

"Andre's process has been a slow one, though I was hoping we were getting close to a breakthrough of some kind. Until you showed up and delivered this dark news, I did expect nothing but forward progress. It has been a long road, and whenever we start to broach the subject of what troubles the boy through journaling, the narrative always reverts to some...tidbit or anecdote about Louis Armstrong. I was hoping that he would grow out of that as he matured. Thirteen is that...gray area. It's a time when we start to feel the first stirrings of young adulthood, but we are still complete children. It can be a time when childhood obsessions fade away."

She cast a glance at Melancon. "Or, they may cement."

"So...just to make sure I'm understanding.

Andre's an obsessive, anxious type? And his obsession is a form of coping with that anxiety?" Felix asked.

"In a manner of speaking," she replied, turning her face to smile at Felix.

"A poor New Orleans boy with a gift for music... right? I mean, that's the connection there, surely? He must see himself when he looks at Armstrong's story," Melancon cut in.

She turned back, the smile fading in an instant, transformed now into a small, derisive smirk pointed at the older man. "Is that your take, Detective? Do you think he simply looks up to Armstrong? Because I think it runs far deeper than that."

The two stared at each other, a frigid electricity passing between them.

"Do you think there are family problems?" Felix asked.

She tapped a pen against her lip, still locked in on Melancon, and shook her head. "Look, I don't think we're getting anywhere here. I'm not able to discuss Andre's family life. I'm afraid I've already said far too much and have broken patient-doctor confidentiality, only due to the fact that you've told me Andre may be in danger. I think, at this point, I'll need you to come back with some kind of warrant."

"Lady, if you have information that could help us find Andre, you need to do the right thing and tell us...

right now! Or what happens to him will be on you," Melancon stammered.

"Unprovoked aggression...weaponized guilt...tell me, Detective, have you seen anyone lately?"

"We'd like to see those journals, please, Doctor," Felix tried. "They could really help us get some insight on the whole situation."

But she'd already crossed her arms.

"I'm afraid I'll ask you to leave now."

"Oh, you will?" Melancon muttered, but he had already stood up and put on his hat. "I thought you shrinks were all about helping people in need?"

Felix pushed him out the door before he could say more.

Out on the sidewalk now, they watched a streetcar pass by and could hear the yelling and screaming of children at their recess in the school across the street.

"That went well," Felix said.

"Let's get downtown," Melancon replied.

They walked briskly towards the car.

"She sure got defensive when we asked about family. Perhaps we should be thinking more towards that angle," Felix said as Melancon revved up the El Camino's raucous engine.

Felix raised an eyebrow. "You think Andre might have been abused?"

The radio came on unbidden, the DJ going on

about the many jazz shows that would be happening that evening.

"You just going to go silent on me, partner?" Felix tried. "Because we've already got one party that doesn't talk, we don't need another."

Melancon grabbed a toothpick and bit into it, peeling out onto St. Charles.

"I don't know...about the abuse," Felix went on. "I don't like the casual way that Melph acted when he found out Andre was missing. And what about his mama? Does he talk to her? He must."

"His stepmom," Melancon finally said.

"Right. He must talk to her?"

Melancon shrugged, letting his blood cool. They rode mostly in tense silence through the midday traffic, the old detective turning the morning over in his head. Finally, they pulled into the parking lot of the downtown station, where Janine was waiting for them.

"You're starting to look like a boss around here," Melancon said to her. He went in for a hug, but she pressed his hands down and shook her head, looking around from side to side.

"Still ashamed of me?"

"Look, we're about to have to let this suspect go."

Melancon found himself nodding. Somehow, he had known it wasn't going to be that easy.

"Forensics came back with the autopsy. It turns out Mr. Adai could not have been shot in the back of the head. Could not have been shot by anyone, in fact, who was riding on the streetcar behind him. The only way would have been if he stopped the car entirely, turned to face his passengers, and was shot by one of them, but since the car was in motion at that time, it's highly unlikely...also..."

A mockingbird landed in the glass-strewn parking lot and pecked at a few loose pebbles of asphalt. All three of them watched it for a moment. Melancon waited until the sickness in his stomach passed.

"There's something else you're going to tell me, isn't there?"

She nodded, squinting in the sunlight that was falling in between the stelae of tall downtown buildings.

"The caliber of the bullet. It's not the nine-millimeter we're used to seeing in an Uptown shooting. Based on the type of injury, forensics is saying that it had to be...larger. Something like a 30-06."

"Like a deer rifle?"

"Like a deer rifle. Like, not the kind of thing you could just pull out of your pocket on a streetcar and then toss in a garbage can. Mr. Adai was no deer. He was a city worker, a husband, and a father."

The cogs turned in his mind.

"Speaking of husband, can you tell me anything more about the stepmom? We may need to talk to her.

Some new developments have occurred...with the boy."

She took a step closer and turned her head to look at Felix. "What about the boy? 'Cause I can't get that uncle of his on the phone and I need to bring that child in for questioning no matter—"

Felix, to his credit, tried to keep it off of his face. But Janine was already becoming fairly gifted in her new position as police detective. She knew the young man would be the weak link when it came to deception. She leaned into him, and there was little David Melancon could do to stop it.

"What is it that you aren't telling me, guys?"

"About the boy...," Felix mumbled.

"He's gone, isn't he?"

"It had nothing to do with us, Janine. That uncle of his just happened to call us and—"

"How the hell did he even get your number?" she demanded.

"Long story," Felix replied, turning his palms up and backing away slowly.

"So, you two detectives come here to tell me that you have no idea where our main witness to a homicide case might be. A young boy at that?"

Melancon put a hand on her shoulder. "We've got a few hunches, Janine, really, but nothing solid yet. Now we find out someone is out there with a deer rifle that may be looking for Andre? Maybe that changes things. But do us a favor, just for a second. Take a deep breath and answer a question for us. Seriously, please. What happens...what would happen if we found the boy right now and brought him to you?"

She bit her lip, looked at him with a bit less anger than before. "Well...if his uncle did lose him, and his stepmom doesn't recover, I'm afraid he will have to enter the custody of the state until his sixteenth...well, let me reconsider that...with Andre's condition...with Andre's inability to communicate...he may be deemed a special case. It's possible he could be rehabilitated, but chances are he would spend quite a few years...institutionalized."

They all three looked at the filthy asphalt underfoot, each of them finding themselves ashamed in their own way, unable to face the pressure and sadness that lurked behind that word. *Institutionalized*. It filled Melancon's thoughts with gray corridors and unsmiling orderlies, with barred windows and state-rationed tiny cups of pills.

"Jesus," he said as the wind swept through the trio and sent the day's pollen swirling around them.

"If you do know where he is, David—look at me, David." Janine's face had gone hard again, though her eyes kept that tepid fondness and understanding. "If you know where he is, or you have him somewhere at one of your partner's...mansions...or some other such foolishness...well, I don't have to tell you. You know how the world works. It won't be just Andre that goes into custody. You could be looking at charges. Kidnapping...I don't know. Just don't do it, okay?"

Melancon started to turn away, started to nod, started to grit his teeth.

"And especially....no matter what you do....don't go to the Lighthouse Behavioral Center in Littlewoods and talk to Lashawn Jones about her missing stepson."

He turned back and stared at her, struck completely silent for once. They nodded at one another, understanding.

"In the meantime, David, I've put a BOLO out on all jazz-related places. Concert venues, museums, things like that. All of them are on the lookout for a little boy with a scar on his neck who doesn't talk and carries a trumpet."

"Do what you think is right, Janine, you always do."

She nodded. "If someone finds him before we do, I hope it's someone with no fashion sense and a bad back."

"And so do I," Melancon said, and the two detectives turned to walk away from her.

TWELVE

Louis Armstrong is seventeen.

Red beans and rice boil in his pot every night, and he throws away his shorts and wears long pants instead. Now he spends his days with a fussy mule, up and down St. Charles, bringing coal for restaurant ovens. At man's work, little Louis is just *Lew-is*: round middle, hard arms, moon face, a smile that stretches from uptown to downtown. Don't get it wrong, though. He's tough in a funny, friendly way—the way some people are tough because they have to be and not because they want to be. Really, there's not a mean bone in his body, but people put money in his hands now instead of throwing it on the street. His voice, when he sings to himself on his rounds, sounds just like the tin buckets of coal being shaken.

The neighborhood has finally turned to look at Louis, turned to listen and to say *here is our big son.*

On the same corner where he used to stuff the quarters into his dipper mouth, a sign appears bearing his name. The name is written small in thin chalk and is under names of bigger headliners, but it's there all the same.

I'm watching the sun come up over the Mississippi. I'm cold, getting very hungry, and I feel smaller than I've ever felt in my life. I want a bowl of beans, a warm bed, and the sound of Daddy's boots on the porch as he heads to work. Small things. They used to be small anyway, but now that they're gone, they seem huge.

Runners jog right by. Barges float. I look way down the river to where it bends away from me, past the bridge and out of sight.

Louis had it right, though. His feet are itching and he starts to look past all those small things that are just there right in front of him. The mule, the long street, the coal-sooty long pants his mama hangs on the line out in the courtyard, the pretty women who try to push aside his horn. Finally, he can do that, can see past all the small to the *vanishing point*. Inside of it he can see the big thing. The feel of it coming, the want of it goes down deeper than rice and beans. Finally, he knows it. Every time he blows his horn, a little more of it goes out of him faster than he can breathe it back in. So he *has* to do something.

The books don't say much about what Louis thought or felt. They just say what he did. But I *know*.

Daddy used to show me the high-water marks on the bank, on the church, on the shed where the street-cars are kept. That green swampy line on everything. He said that line was a limit to all possibilities. He said that I wouldn't understand until I had gotten to be taller than the watermark Freret Street and north. He used to show me the old spray paint Xs where the bodies were found on houses that still hadn't been torn down. He would show it to me and say that it would come again. That everything big here would be made quickly small. That we would be forgotten. *The water,* he would say. But I don't think he was talking about just water. Not really. When I read about Louis Armstrong being seventeen, I know what Daddy was *really* trying to tell me. Louis was like the roots of the oak trees on St. Charles and how they bust up and break the banquettes when they get too big. Sometimes the thoughts inside my head feel just like that, too.

An old man comes stumbling down the Riverwalk and right by me. He's got a scruffy red beard and long stringy hair, and he's got a dog with him. It's some kind of a mutt and it has a bad limp. Along the side of it, you can see the rib bones poking out. The man's face is also thin and dirty, but he's the first person all morning that has turned his eyes to look at me. When he does, I feel scared, but also ashamed, and also happy that I'm not alone at that very moment because the thoughts I'm thinking about being scared of just this one man are so much easier than the ones about being afraid of everything else in the world.

"Good morning, young man. I don't suppose you have a dollar so I can get myself something to eat?"

I still have a single from the Big Waif Brass Band, crumpled up in my pocket. It's all I have, dry now. I pull it out, smooth it across the edge of the bench a few times, and reach it out to him.

He looks down at the bill and then behind me, and then all around me, looking now at everything there *except* for me. I can see that something about the bill has scared him, so I stick it out again an inch further this time and try to smile.

"You out here alone?" he says.

I nod my head.

"You run off?"

I nod at him again.

The old man takes the bill in his wrinkled hand, holds it up to the sunlight quickly and then folds it and puts it into the front pocket of his shirt, which is the kind that lumberjacks wear in cartoons. He looks at the scar on my neck for a minute.

Then he sits down next to me on the bench and is quiet for a really long time, not saying anything.

"My old man was a real bastard," he finally says and looks at me sideways.

I don't say anything.

"You will be alright," he says to me.

I nod my head at him as if to say thank you. After a long while, he stands up and walks on down the river.

I'm still cold and I'm hungry but now I'm sure something big is about to come. Not only is it coming but it is big and it is coming today. The sun is fully up and I watch the old man getting smaller and smaller as he follows the river upstream and away from me, taking my last bill with him. I can feel it, deep inside my bones. Something is going to happen. It may be a bad thing that happens, but at least there will be no more waiting for it.

I make it down to the café. It has a wide outdoor area with at least a hundred tables, all filled with people from other places. Even the waiters, their uniforms, the way they move—all of it seems like it is from somewhere else. But it's a place I've been many times before. Daddy used to take me here once in a while. I try to pick out which tables we sat at, I try to remember what we had, but then I remember there is only one thing on the menu and that is beignets.

I pick out a particular table where I think Daddy and I must have sat a few years ago. I don't know why I remember the exact table, but I'm sure, as soon as I sit down at it, that this is the very one. I look across from where I'm sitting, over the piles of crumpled napkins and coffee cup lids and powdered sugar. I look down at the empty chair where Daddy sat back then.

"You probably don't understand why I'm being like this."

I remember him saying that.

"You have to remember what happens when that train starts to roll. You just a boy, Andre. But you won't be one forever. Whatever happens now is going to stick on you the rest of your life, like mud on your boots that there is no scraping off."

He looked sad, tired. Or maybe it's my memory that is tired. I think he was still wearing his uniform. I try to pretend he is still sitting there, talking to me. But there is nothing but a patch of pale sunlight in the chair now, coming just under the awning.

"One day you will remember. You will just choose to remember," he told me. "When that happens I want you right here with me, not off someplace in New York City."

I try to keep Daddy there in my mind's eye, to finish remembering what he said to me, but I can't because I'm too hungry. He fades away because all I can smell is the frying dough and the coffee now and I start to realize how food is such a tiny little thing until you don't have it, and then it is a huge thing, the *only thing*. I wonder if I'm going to end up looking like that old man's dog, a waif with my bones poking out. There are pigeons at my feet, and they are all pecking like mad, and I guess I must know how they feel, too. Everything in the world is hungry.

I'm sitting and watching all of the people come and go, watching them bite into the soft little wads of dough, and suddenly I have an idea. I can't say the idea is original or special really. In fact, it's more of like a memory from the times I've been here before.

I brush myself off a little bit. But no matter how hard or fast I brush, some of the dirt and grime that comes from sleeping under an old house just won't come off. I pull my horn out of my bag. I find a box in the trash can.

Now I'm standing on the cobblestones with my horn out in front of me, shaking because of what I'm about to do. A whole mess of people are sitting in the café, talking and eating. I want to say something charming and gravelly to get their attention, I want to be loud and big. Of course, they aren't paying me any mind. Then I remember that I'm not charming or gravelly, I'm a house-sleeping-under waif.

"There is no shame in being small," Daddy said, sitting at that table right there. I finally remember that part.

I put the horn to my lips and I blow. I hit that high C. I blow so hard and high that I can feel the seam of my lip burst. It fills my mouth with a taste that isn't much different than the taste of coins—iron and copper and other important things. I blow that one long note and I put everything bad in the world in one end and out the other comes everything good. I look around and the people have got real quiet and are staring at me, so I let loose again with a twisting high note. By the time I go into the chorus of "Saints," people are clapping along and whistling and smiling at me. I feel myself start to rock from side to side. I'm slurping the blood down in between blows as best I can so that the people won't go from fun to concerned. A woman with a sweater tied around her waist prods a blond-headed little boy over to my box and I watch him drop a five. Three other people come up with bills and a few other come up with change.

I just finish a song and am about to start another when an old man grabs me by the arm. He is dark, with a flat cap and gray whiskers and a strange look on his face.

"What...the...hell you think...you're doing?" he stammers. He's so angry that he can't seem to get his words out straight. He's missing a tooth on the right side of his mouth, and there's a yellow tint to the whites of his eyes.

I raise my horn up to him, trying to show him what it is I think I'm doing, but that doesn't help.

"You can't just be...moving spot. This sidewalk's... got three grown men in line waiting for it, and you just come up and start to...start to blow? Now how does that work?"

A few of the tourists are watching now, and I notice that the old man is pretending to smile and getting most of his words out under his breath, like. He takes a step towards me and—

She comes in between us suddenly. Where did she come from? Out from the crowd walking by on the streets, no warning. But somehow, she knows just what's happening and is ready for it. Right away she raises her arms over her head. She's in the face of the old man, yelling at him, screaming. The tourists in the café stare hard and then not at all, looking down seriously at newspapers and cell phones.

She wins the fight before it even happens—the type of tough you can tell is because she enjoys it, because that is how she is. The old man can see it right away too, and maybe her small size makes it so that she can act that tough and get away with it. He doesn't look scared so much as confused, out of ideas. She is screaming at him and I can see the spit landing on his face, but he only stands there bug-eyed and quiet. She finishes with him and turns to me and yanks my arm hard, pulling me across the street. Then she marches me into a quiet area of Jackson Square Park, pushes me down on a bench.

"Andre," she says.

I look right down into her dark eyes and get pulled backwards. Her eyes are a forest around me. Her eyes are quiet. Her eyes are like the eyes of some animal slowly dying on the forest floor. Those eyes look up at me, shocked and afraid but also accepting the vanishing point that's coming one way or another.

And her lips? What is that color? The shade is like the wine you see people sipping in restaurant windows. It is smeared across a large, gum-chewing mouth.

Her face is the one from my dreams. The one from the crowd on Frenchman Street.

"You know me, don't you, boy?"

I shake my head. She smacks her gum and lets out a little chuckle. She has one arm on my leg and is pinning me to the bench. She must feel the muscle in my leg flinch. It wants to run. She looks down at me and tightens her grip a bit, shuffling forward on her haunches. People in the park are playing frisbee, guitar. Children are running circles around Andrew Jackson on his horse. We are a woman and a child in a park and I realize no one knows that this isn't normal.

"Say it."

I lower my eyes, my head. I think about the gun in my backpack.

"You know that old man that was about to take your head off? I hope you got a good, long look at him. You saw how dirty he was. You saw the missing teeth, the crooked back. I hope you got a good look at him, Andre."

There are a few police officers walking through the

park now. I look at them. She uses her fingers to turn my chin back towards her.

"Because that is going to be *you*. That old man is just how you are going to turn out, if you don't listen to me."

I stare at her.

She puts a second hand on me now, up on my forearm. I can feel her long nails pressing into my skin. She holds me tighter as she talks, and it hurts.

"Andre."

She's squeezing so hard I start to flinch, and it feels like the skin on my arm will burst.

"You remembering? Maybe you don't remember. But try. The pine trees, the horses, the creek."

The pain of her tight, pointed grip hurts me too bad. I can't focus. That color on her lips. What is that called? Where do I know it from? Why am I so filled with terror?

I try to pull away, softly at first and then as hard as I can. She frowns at me, slaps me across the face so hard that the blood in my mouth, which is from blowing the horn too hard and not from the slap, comes flying out. Only she doesn't know what it's from and must think she has hurt me worse than she has, because she immediately bites her lip, loosens her grip a bit, and looks over her shoulder at the police.

When I feel her hand go soft, I pull with all my force and suddenly break free. But the first thing I do with freedom is fall off the bench from the momentum. She stands up, but I manage to get to my feet before she can grab me a second time.

I don't look back at her, but I can picture exactly what her face might look like. That wine color. The eyes like an animal dying on the forest floor. One of my shoes falls off, but I don't bend down to pick it up.

I just run. I'm out of the park gates and into the groups of people in seconds, deciding that I'm not going to stop, not now and not ever. I decide that running is my life now. I pass Decatur Street and look down it both ways, wondering where it is that I might go.

Something in my feet makes the choice for me, and in the next moment I'm bouncing up the steps to the Riverwalk. I can feel the horn in my backpack, the rim of it pressing into the skin on my neck just as cold and hard as her nails bit into my arm. Because of the levee, I come up to one of the highest places in the whole Quarter. I can stop and look back, look down. I see the top of her head.

I see her talking to the police, I see her pointing at me.

I keep running, down to the little area of tents and boxes set up along the big rocky bank of the Mississippi.

"What you running from, boy?"

It's the old man from earlier, the one with the

hungry dog that I gave my last dollar to. He's standing in front of the open flap of a tent.

I point behind me. A big, strong, arm-waving point.

He nods at me, waves me towards the inside of his tent. I don't have time to think about it. I dive in head-first and crawl into the corner.

THIRTEEN

It was midday, the sun perched high up in the cloudless sky. A hungry line of people stood in the open doorway of the little restaurant on Annunciation Street, letting the cool wind mix in and dilute the burnt-grease smell of the deep fryer.

Melancon loved this place, had loved it since he was a boy. But today he only poked at his food, sipping his root beer and trying to keep his eyes off the frosty mugs of the real deal being poured up at the bar. He might have had little appetite, but the place was packed to capacity, and through the open kitchen he could watch three generations deep in the weeds, laboring over egg wash and cold fixings and bread knives. He gave his young partner the chance to get a few bites of po'boy in, trying his best to manage the queasiness rising up in his gut. Melancon might have been troubled, worn thin and even a little sick to his stomach, but the youth had to eat.

"Weird day," Felix said in between mouthfuls of fluffy French bread.

Melancon watched him as he put the sandwich down and fiddled with Andre's cell phone, just as he'd been doing the whole morning. The young man's shoulders had sunk a few degrees, and there were dark circles under his eyes. He'd been picking at his finger-nails, a sure sign that his zesty energy was taking a darker turn. Even his eating seemed distracted—he'd left bits of batter and bread crumbs spread across the table.

"I don't see anything else on Andre's phone that looks helpful," Felix said, putting the device back down, just a little too hard, on the table, and drawing a few eyes from the seats next to them. He took another monstrous bite of the po'boy and shook his head while his jaw worked at it.

"That's okay, Felix. Remember when the uncle asked us to mail it to him?"

Melancon ripped the page out of his notepad and put it on top of the cell phone, poking it with his index finger three times for emphasis.

"I think it is time we stopped by that address and dropped the thing off personally. Family members might be our best chance. Talk to Melph, check him out while we're up here. Then, we head east to have a chat with the stepmama," Melancon said.

"You think Melph will talk to us? He's liable to tell us to get fucked, especially if he knows we suspect him in the slightest...which...do we?"

"I don't know, kid. Everyone is a suspect right now, since I'm not working with much to go on. Though a lot of times, with things like this, it *is* in the family."

Felix brushed some crumbs off of his shirtfront, leaned back in the chair, and raised his chin a bit.

"You're right, it might be our best bet at figuring this out. It's either that or cruise around and pray Andre pops up on some street corner."

Melancon nodded, wrapped his untouched roast beef up in the greasy paper, and made for the door. He tipped his hat to the old matriarch of the place as he squeezed between the influx of hungry patrons lined up at the front.

"You need to eat, old man," his partner said to him once they were back out in the sunshine.

"I can't think straight with a crowd like that, much less eat."

The young detective pulled out his own buzzing phone. Melancon knew well who it would be, once again, and he tried to tune out the conversation that had been repeating itself most of that tense morning as he made his way back to his car.

"Yes, Tomás....Yes, we're doing our best.... Yes....

Okay, but....Alright. We're going to find him. We have to eat, Tomás.... Yes.... Okay. Just give us a little more time. We're going straight to the family now....Yes, we will. I'll tell him to be careful."

The day had noticeably warmed, the crepe myrtle buds falling on everything. Melancon stopped just a minute to appreciate it all before he swung open the complaining door of the El Camino.

"You reckon the stepmama will be wearing a strait-jacket when we see her?" Felix asked, pulling open the passenger door.

Melancon shook his head, yelled over the roaring sound of the old engine. "Shrinks will put you away for almost anything these days."

"Man, you really don't like psychologists, do you?"

Melancon shrugged his shoulders, shook his bare head, and then tightened his grip on the old leather steering wheel.

"No, I certainly do not."

Halfway down Carrollton, Melancon pulled over at a familiar crossroads and killed the engine. "Let's check the crime scene while we're over here. Then we pop in on Uncle, unexpected like," he said.

They stepped out by the corner of Oak Street. There was little to show of the bloody events that had transpired here, only a few days prior. Some tattered police tape, mashed into the mud of the neutral ground by the shoes of passing commuters. One of the short, stubby palmetto trees the city had planted was now sadly uprooted and lying on its side in the Bermuda grass, but otherwise it was business as usual for this busy place.

They stood out under the oak boughs, glancing around, taking it in.

Melancon tried his best to imagine the horror of the thing. The peaceful, jostling ride beforehand. Then the sudden crack of a high-caliber rifle. The echo such a weapon would have had in this place, during a commuting hour, was unmistakable. Hundreds of people would have heard it. How far away would they have heard it from? Over the cars, the streetcar, the children playing in the nearby yard, the mocking birds in the trees, the coffee shop chatter next door, the church bells ringing, they would have heard—

The church bells ringing.

Melancon was seized by that sudden clarity of thought that had yet stubbornly refused to join his hair and his strong back in abandoning him. About fifty yards down Carrolton Street there was a large Catholic Church that the old detective knew well. Although it was far removed from the little neighborhood steeple he'd attended as a boy, here was a building of some repute among Catholics in the city. It had stood there for near two hundred years, even back when the "city of Carrolton" was still a separate thing from New Orleans—a piece of the local landscape and a common place for christenings, marriages, funerals and the like. It had been a decade since Melancon had been inside, but he still remembered the delicately painted faces of the saints looking down at you from the ceiling of the prominent dome in the front. And it had bell towers, a pair of them that flanked the dome. He looked up at them, standing with his arms akimbo in the neutral ground. The sun, intense now and penetrating the oak canopy, made it hard to study the aged piece of architecture as closely as he would have liked. So, he went closer.

With his eyes adjusted and the distance shortened, he was able to study the high perches. Twin spires, one of them quite close and very clearly overlooking the streetcar line. They were the approximate height of a third-story building and made of solid old stone.

Felix was looking, too.

"Sniper's nest?" the young man asked.

"I can't imagine anything else. Can't imagine a person standing out here where we are, in the neutral ground, firing a high-powered rifle, and then being able to just casually stroll away without being noticed, can you?"

Felix squinted up at it, a hand over his eyes. "What about all the porches around here? Some of them look like they might work. Maybe a second-story window?"

"Possible, but what kind of an idiot would come out on his porch and murder someone in broad daylight? Doesn't make sense. I don't see many windows with a good angle either."

They approached the base of the nearest bell tower, which was surrounded by a little sparse patch of grass. The main cathedral had a large series of concrete stairs leading up to it, making the whole structure quite elevated by the pancake standards of Uptown. Melancon could still make out, only just faintly, the green high-water mark on the exterior walls of the tower, just at about his eye level.

The old detective edged closer, right up to the base of the spire, where he looked straight up. A good fifty feet at least, he reckoned. He looked down at the ground beneath him, at his now dusty shoes. He bent down and ran his fingers against a few errant blades of grass.

"There are cigarette butts here," Felix said.

The young man was standing a few feet away by the Carrolton facing side of the bell tower's wall, down on his haunches now, picking at little bits of cotton littering the ground.

Melancon took a visual measurement. The spot was a bit too far away from the sidewalk to be so littered. He looked up, then back down to the ground.

"Hand me one of those, will you, kid? Damn back is about to have a fit."

Felix plucked one of the butts up with apparent distaste and handed it to the old detective.

"B&H."

Melancon only pretended to read it. The letters were crumpled and his eyes were no longer that sharp. But he knew the make from the color of the text, the circumference, the smell. A strange thing to easily recognize, he knew, but there was no mistaking what was always there at the lamp table next to his long-gone granny's easy chair.

"My grandmama used to smoke these. Minty little thin things. The kind of thing elegant old ladies used to smoke, back when old folks smoking was the norm."

"There sure are a lot of them here."

"Almost like someone up there was nervous, but I doubt it was an elegant old lady," Melancon said and glanced up at the tower again.

"Can we go up?" Felix asked.

"I don't think so, Felix. Last time you had me snooping around a holy place, it didn't work out so well, remember? Anyway, this might be nothing. Or, it might be something. But we got bigger fish to fry right now. We chase this rabbit, we're going to lose the other one. I'll let Janine know about this, and she'll tell the forensics guys. Don't touch anything else."

"Right, find the kid first, before Mr. de Valencia has an aneurism."

Melancon nodded.

Five minutes later they were pulling up in front of an orange bungalow with a sagging porch, deep in the

Seventeenth. The streets were mostly empty, aside from an old, rail-thin man who was planting a small tree in his front yard. Down the road they could hear music coming out of a small corner store. The roads were bad, even for here, and Melancon could find no place to pull over his rust bucket other than a pool of water about ten feet across. Both he and Felix had wet feet by the time they opened the little wooden gate in front of Melph's place.

They were up on the low-slung porch, looking things over. He let Felix do the knocking while he took a bit of a snoop around. No car in the driveway, doubtful if he'd be home. And why would he come to the door, anyway? But they had to try. Over in one corner of the porch was a lawn chair, and next to it a table, and on that table an ashtray.

"Knock, knock," Felix said to the closed door. "Anybody home?"

Melancon looked down into the ashtray.

There was no mistaking the butts.

"Felix," he said in a quiet voice. "Look!"

He pinched up one of the butts.

"B&H," he said. There was some sort of a smudge on the butt, but Melancon couldn't quite make out what it was.

Felix knocked once again, harder this time.

"Well, I guess he ain't home, and what y'all want with him, anyway?" said a female voice from the porch next door. It was a space that shared an intimate closeness with this one, and yet the two detectives had hardly noticed a woman sitting there, reclining in her bathrobe with a petite little lapdog in her arms.

She looked to be in her midthirties, was broad-faced and pretty. Her short, thick legs stuck out from her bathrobe, and she was sipping a tall cup of something.

"We're trying to find a lost boy. A boy whose last known whereabouts were here. Andre Adai, did you know him?"

"Sure, I know Andre. Weird little kid, but at least he behaved himself. Shit. Not like my kids."

"You didn't see anything, did you, miss?" Melancon said, taking his hat in his hands. "Andre has been missing for a few days now and we've got no idea where to find him."

She smiled, looked down the street and put her lapdog down on the ground.

"Sorry."

"What can you tell us about Melph?" Felix asked. He extended his credentials across the porch railing, but she didn't look at them.

"He's fine. Tough type of guy, but fine. He was in the war, you know."

Melancon nodded, turned to his partner. "You think he's out looking for Andre?"

"You still didn't answer my question. What do you

want with Melph?" the woman said, a little more demanding this time.

"Does Melph have a woman?"

She gave him a strange look. The little dog let out a few yaps and clicked its nails around the porch. "Ask him yourself," she said and pointed to the street.

A green Explorer had pulled up onto a grassy spot, elevated above the wide puddle.

Melph stepped out and lowered himself slowly down onto the wet St. Augustine, surveying the situation on his porch. He seemed to understand it immediately, or else his face simply didn't register any detectible amount of surprise, shock or offense. He quickly strode up the steps and, going right in between the two detectives, jammed a key into his front door.

"You seen Andre?" Felix asked the back of him.

Melph bent down and picked up a few pieces of mail at his threshold, then went inside his house without a word—but he left the door wide open behind him.

The two detectives shared a nervous glance with each other.

"Go on," the neighbor woman said from her porch. "I'm sure he don't mind."

They stood on the threshold between the porch and a darkened living room that smelled faintly of marijuana and wet cypress.

Melph was moving around noisily in the attached

kitchen. "She's right," he called, "come on if you're coming."

Melancon glanced back to where his El Camino was parked in its dirty pool of water, crammed between the blocky SUV and a full can of garbage, just behind. No chance for a quick escape there, were things to suddenly go sour.

He caught Felix give him a slight nod. The boy could be a risk taker when things got to this point.

Melancon stuck his head in and craned his neck, which let him see just into the kitchen.

Melph was standing over the sink with his back to them. Melancon put his hand on his holster and stepped inside.

"You going to shoot me in my own house?" Melph said, raising his head from the sink.

Melancon got a clear look at the man as he turned to face the two detectives, a glass of water in his bony hand. Tall and thin and handsome. The kind of guy that women go crazy for—the muscles, the tattoos, the rakish dreadlocks slung across his brow. He had a tiredness around his eyes as he lifted the glass to his lips and downed the whole of it in a series of thirsty gulps.

"Hadn't planned on doing any shooting. But there have been some bullets flying lately. Can you blame us for being a little jumpy?"

"Hey, you came looking for me. I'm the one that

should be jumpy." Melph wiped his mouth dry with a bare arm and approached them, bending slightly down to get on the eye level with the old detective. "But I've been around too many flying bullets to be jumpy, Detective. You look like you've dodged a few yourself."

Melph glanced sideways at Felix with a dismissive smirk, and turned back to his kitchen. "No luck. How about you, find him yet?" he asked over his shoulder.

The two detectives looked at each other in silent tension.

"Answer me this, then," Melph went on. "See, I always thought, and this is probably just from picking up false intel from the TV, but I always thought that private detectives needed to be *hired* by someone in order to take a case. So, who the hell hired y'all? Because I know Lashawn didn't. She ain't all there at the moment, I'm afraid."

"Some cases we take on a pro bono basis. This is one of them," Melancon replied coolly.

"Pro bono, eh?"

"It means—" Felix started to say.

"I know what it means, kid."

Melancon used the awkward silence that followed to take a look around the living room, in which he was still standing, very much on guard. There was nothing unusual about it for a man in his midthirties, nothing overtly sinister, except that it was quite clearly the home of a dyed-in-the-wool bachelor—flat-screen TV bigger and nicer than any other object in the room, a picture of the Saints running back as the sole wall decoration, a kitschy statue of Bob Marley and a mason jar of pot sitting squarely on the coffee table in lieu of the books on architecture and gardening and other such flourishes of taste you might find purposely smattered around a married man's home.

"Andre," Melph said, pulling a beer from the fridge and popping the top off against the kitchen island. He took another long drink. "You know, sometimes I thank God for certain things."

"Like what?" Melancon asked, shifting his focus and taking one more step towards the kitchen.

Melph chucked to himself over his bottle. "It might confuse you."

"Try me."

"For example," Melph said, pointing his beer finger at the two detectives, "just the other day I thanked God to be just smart enough. You know what that means?"

Melph looked heavily at Felix as he joined the two detectives in the living room, placing his long frame down on the couch. "I'm no genius, mind, but I got a decent enough head on my shoulders. And that's the important part. *Decent enough.* See, you...I already know what you thinking about that boy. You would call a mind like Andre's *gifted*, wouldn't you? As if being that kind of way was some kind of...reward. A gift. Shit."

He threw his feet up onto the coffee table and stretched out.

"It isn't a gift. It isn't a reward at all. It's a curse. God made somebody that smart...like as a curse. Andre knows it, too. Shit, when I was his age I was just smart enough. Smart enough to be a kid. Chased every girl on the block, hung out with boys who would have died for me in a split second. All 'cause I wasn't Andre's kind of smart. Because that boy is cursed with intelligence...smart as he is, don't know how to do anything except blow that damn horn."

"That's why we have to find him," Felix said, his voice going hostile and sour. "And why we have to find who shot his daddy so we can send that bastard to Angola State Penitentiary."

Melph smiled, sipped his beer. "Andre ain't going to be found unless he wants to be. But I think you know that already. That's why you're here with no Andre and no clue, isn't it?"

"So, you haven't seen him?" Melancon pressed.

"What's it look like? Do you *detect* any thirteen-year-old Rain Man–looking motherfuckers around here?"

"So, you just lost him, is that it?"

Melph said nothing, but the old detective was sure

he saw a look of shame pass over those handsome features, if only for a brief moment.

"And no idea who is responsible for this murder, I suppose?"

"Shit. Nope."

"You wouldn't tell us anyway, even if you knew, though, would you?"

"Probably not. Because you not even them people, anyway. You just a couple of guys getting your wet feet all over my rug."

They looked down, embarrassed, backing off slightly.

Melancon let a heavy silence hang for a long moment between them. Then he nodded to his young partner, who was beginning to go a bit red around the ears. "Well, sorry for wasting your time."

Out on the porch, Melancon pulled at his belt and spoke in the most casual voice he could command, calling back into the darkness of the bungalow.

"Say, Melph, I heard you were in the armed services. What was it that you did over...well where were you?"

"Iraq. Afghanistan," he replied, standing up and coming to his door, squinting out into the sunlight.

"And you were Army?"

"Marines."

"Impressive. And what did you do as a Marine?"

Melancon was standing on the stoop now, hands on his hips. "Or are you even allowed to even say?"

Melph came out onto the porch and leaned over the railing to pack his cigarettes against his wrist.

"For detectives, you two damn sure don't detect much," he said, glancing down the street and lighting himself a smoke with an old Zippo.

Melancon thought a moment. "Hey, can I get one of those cigarettes? I'm trying to quit, but my damn nerves are just shot to hell over this business."

A long arm reached down from the porch and delivered one of the tailor-mades.

Melancon was able to sneak a quick glance down at it, but that wasn't necessary. The feeling of it between his thumb and pointer finger was all wrong—too thick and substantial. Definitely not B&H. The smell from Melph's lit one, heavy and tar-filled and masculine, confirmed it.

"Need a light?" Melph asked.

"No, I got one in the car, thanks."

"So, what did you do in the Marines?" Felix repeated.

Melph blew out smoke and didn't reply.

Melancon snapped his fingers. "You know what, Felix, I do have a friend downtown...and you know... she has a friend who has access to records like that. NPRC, right? I think it's form 180..."

"Sniper," Melph said. "I was a sniper."

He flicked ash down over the porch railing that wafted over and landed on Felix's shirt.

Melancon nodded. "Sniper, eh? I'd wager you have a story or two to tell. And, hey, maybe you'll show us your rifle collection before this is all done and dusted, what do you say?"

Once again, Melph did not reply. He snubbed out his cigarette and looked at them.

"Oh, I almost forgot," Melancon said, "we came here to bring you Andre's phone."

The old man reached inside his coat pocket, but before he could pull out the device, Melph was already shaking his head.

"You know what, keep it, partner," Melph said, and without another word, he went inside his house and closed the door.

"Y'all leave that handsome young man alone, hear?" the neighbor lady called after them, her lapdog yapping, as the two detectives tiptoed their retreat through the deep puddle on Leonidas Street.

FOURTEEN

Louis Armstrong is seventeen and has never left New Orleans.

He stands on a wharf looking out over the river. Skyscrapers, mountains, heavy snow, the pyramids, the Eiffel Tower: these are just some of the things he hasn't seen yet. Right now, he is wearing his best suit, his mama's cornbread wrapped up in a handkerchief and stuffed in his jacket pocket. He has made up his mind to never tote another bucket of coal in his life. He doesn't even know what a hero he is.

The same sound that I'm hearing right now, he hears it, too.

It comes rolling down between the streets and bouncing off of walls and throws itself out over the springtime Mississippi. *The Calliope.* That's because they let the steam from the steam ship be put to use. They don't waste it. Instead, they let it go up through a pipe organ on top of the ship, where it makes a beautiful, holy sound. It plays "Oh! Susanna" and "Saints" and "Dixie" and—

Louis hears it and he smiles, taps his foot against the wharf planks. It makes him less afraid, that this is the sound he will be leaving to. Music can make you brave. He knows it, even if he doesn't speak the words. The river doesn't start here but it does end here. Everything is flowing and floating down to this final *vanishing point.* Louis will never come back to New Orleans.

Sure, he will visit. They will have a parade for him when he steps off of the train on Canal Street a decade later. The whole city will rise up in pride and joy at their great son's return. He'll even be King of Zulu. But he will never *really* come back. Instead, he takes this place with him. Stuffs it in his pocket. He will sing its songs, dance its dances, beg his every wife to cook its foods and add its spices to every meal. For the rest of his life, he will do that. He'll play over-the-top, jazzy cats in Hollywood movies. He'll perform our way, talk our way, and when he gets up in some faraway place, standing with his handkerchief in front of maybe a king and queen, he'll blow New Orleans straight into his brass, and the sound of it will make the world tremble with happiness and awe and love.

But when he dies, he will be buried in a different type of dirt. Not this red Mississippi sand. He'll die in

New York and be buried in that faraway cold and stony ground.

Not here.

But right now, seventeen-year-old Louis Armstrong is putting his first foot down on that long road that will take him around the world and back again a dozen times.

Because Louis has been hired to step on board a steamship, just like the one I'm hiding in now, to go upriver all the way north. He'll play songs for rich people, out on a pleasure cruise, and he will leave his home behind. It's the first step towards the big thing, the huge thing, that will make everything else seem small.

One day, he'll be on the cover of *Life*. His voice will be put on a gold record and sent out into the cosmos. A postage stamp will show his face blowing a horn.

But right now, he is just a kid stepping onto a boat.

Just like me.

I hid in the smelly tent for an hour, trembling, hoping not to be found out. Finally, the homeless man opened the zipper and said, "You can come out, kid, those cops are gone off down the road."

I crawled out and stood in the sunshine, which had somehow changed the way everything looked from just an hour ago. It felt gentler now, covering the whole Quarter softly, gleaming off the rooftops and statues. I could hear the old toothless man had taken my spot by the café and was playing a sleepy tune on his sax.

"You want to get out of here if you're being hunted, just for a little while. They'll lose interest pretty quick. Unless you killed somebody. You didn't kill nobody, did you, kid?"

I shook my head.

"There's a spot, right down there by the big riverboat, you see it? You hide there, and wait. Then, when you get a chance, sneak into that door where they load up the food. The boat comes back here again, after a while, but no one will be able to bother you for a few hours if you stay in the storage hold. It's real warm too, and you can hear the music when they cut the engine."

I looked down where he was pointing, saw a crowd of people milling around in front of an old paddle wheel riverboat.

We walked down there together, and once we got in front of the crowd, the old man bowed real low and said in a booming voice, "Behold, the greatest blues singer in all the world, King Oliver."

The old man pulled out a harmonica and began to blow it up and down the scales. His dog, on cue, started howling high and doleful.

Everyone gathered around, although it really didn't sound that nice. I guess the dog was pretty cute, and he could keep up with the harmonica. No one was paying attention and I just walked right in and hid behind some bags of rice.

Now I'm huddled in the dark. The storage room is warm and nice and quiet except for the beautiful sound of the calliope playing those old songs. The muscles in my body start to relax for the first time in a few days, and I suddenly realize how very tired I am. Every bit of me is sore and worn out and I have little pains and bruises all over me.

For some reason, I decide to pull one of the bullet shells out of the pocket of the army jacket and look at it. There's only just enough light in the room for me to make out the outline of the thing. I know it's just where the powder goes, and that the killing bit, which is missing, is actually—

I squeeze the thing in my hand, trying to crush it, trying to ball it up into a little crumpled nothing like you might do with a piece of tinfoil. But I know it's made to deal with explosions bigger than any I can ever make, no matter how hard I try.

I wonder where did they bury my daddy. I hope it was in the Seventeenth Ward. I hope it was right near his home. I hope it wasn't in some faraway cold dirt. Or maybe they burned him up. Maybe they—

I let things go for a minute, put the shell back in its place in my pocket, and fall asleep with my head laid on one of the big bags of rice.

A while later, I'm woken up by a terrible sound.

It's like a dragon in the room just next to me, roaring something awful. It must be the engine room that the old man mentioned, but knowing what it is doesn't make it any better. My ears are on fire, and I can't hear anything, not the lovely calliope, not even my own thoughts. The sound is so painful, I have to stick my fingers in my ears until I can muffle that sound just a little bit, so that I can start to think again.

There's no way I can stay. No way I can ignore this poison in my ears being so close. So, with my ears plugged against the pain, I make a plan in my head. I will go up on the deck, pretend I'm just another traveler enjoying a pleasure cruise. I'll stand up in the fresh air and smell the river and hear the calliope and watch the happy families who have daddies still with them. I'll make believe I'm one of them, listen to the calliope, and I'll think about when Louis Armstrong left his home on a boat just like this.

The door to the storage room is heavy and metal, but it opens with a creaking sound. Thankfully, the engine covers up that, as well as my footsteps against the metal floor. No one could possibly hear me as I come out into a long hallway. At the end of the hallway I see a set of stairs that has sunshine falling on it.

Outside the sky is blue and brilliant and I see one of the most beautiful sights I've ever seen. That's because of what is called *perspective*. New Orleans, which is a place that seems so large when you've spent your whole life standing inside of it, seems small now. The river stretches out on all sides of us and I finally know just what a big river it is. The tall buildings of downtown are a small little clump of dominoes now, and I can make out the top of the Superdome sitting just like a marble between them.

I realize that the calliope has stopped playing now and that the music I'm hearing is coming from a live band. I'm on one of the middle decks, and so I take another set of stairs up to the top deck, where the sunshine hits the top of my head and a group of men in pressed white shirts are playing some swinging Dixieland-type music.

New Orleans gets smaller and smaller on the far bank of the river, and I wonder at what point it will disappear into a vanishing point and what that will be like for me.

I find a chair that's right near the railing in the sunshine. It's warm now and I just sit there enjoying the music and thinking about—

I feel a hand grip my shoulder. A man in a uniform. Not quite a police uniform, but halfway there. His hold on me is strong.

"Andre Adai?" he asks.

I don't say anything, I just look him in his eyes to see if there is any hate for me there, any anger. I can't see any. What I do see is pride. He's proud he found me, like I'm a seventy-pound fish he has caught. I know this is bad. He knows my name and I can see him carry me into the station, where everyone gathers around. He will slap me down on the desk and stand back and puff his chest and let everyone take photos.

I stand up, and when I do I twist and manage to get loose. He takes a few slow steps towards me, and now my back is to the railing that faced the small city a few minutes ago but now just faces a bunch of old run-down factories along the shore.

"Come on, kid," he says and tries to make a fake laugh. "The jig is up. I'm not the bad guy here. They gave me this picture of you, see?" He holds out a Polaroid, which I can't see because the sun is hitting my eyes. "They told me about that scar on your neck." He points. "Told me you loved jazz, and you loved riverboats, and that you might show up one day. And if you did, I needed to call it in. They said you ran off and have everyone worried sick. Don't worry, you aren't in trouble. You're just lost."

I know right where I am. I'm on the Mississippi River, floating right away. I know that in another hour the riverboat will turn and I will be brought right back, and that they will be waiting for me—the NOPD, everyone will be waiting to grab me.

The band keeps right on playing.

I take another backstep towards the railing. I hoist

up my backpack tight against my arms. Music can make you brave.

The man in uniform takes another step towards me now, and his smile has gone all nervous and unsure.

I've never been a good swimmer, but the shore is so close I'm certain it will be okay. But I also know about the Mississippi River, because I grew up right beside it. I know that young men full of beer try to swim across it every year and that it sucks them down into its depths. When they get spat out, they're fifty miles away, floating out into the ocean. If they're lucky, a fisherman is able to drag them out of the water so their family gets a funeral. I know that the water is so muddy that if you go under just one foot, then no one can see you at all. I know there are catfish lurking at the bottom the size of great white sharks, and if you see one you will never go back in the water again for your entire life.

But maybe all that isn't as bad as it sounds.

I turn.

I face the river and look down at it.

"Kid?" the riverboat man says.

FIFTEEN

"A fucking Marine sniper."

"Yeah, I heard the man, Felix."

"Did you?"

"Yeah."

"Wasn't the guy who shot Kennedy a Marine?"

"Something like that."

"A Marine sniper, with the same kind of obscure cigarettes in *his* ashtray, on *his* porch, as the ones we found at the base of the bell tower overlooking the crime scene, where a man was clearly sniped."

"But he doesn't smoke them," Melancon said and pulled Melph's cigarette from behind his ear to hand to his worked-up young partner.

They were rolling along in the El Camino, burning east on smooth federal roads. With the sun behind them and the humidity chilled from the air, they could see for miles.

Felix turned the papery thing in his hand, rolled it between his thumb and pointer finger. "He could have smoked an off-brand in front of you to throw you off. Or maybe he smokes more than one type of cigarette, depending on his mood. Doesn't mean anything."

"Neither does being a sniper. It's all circumstantial so far. Not even enough for a warrant, I don't think."

The young man fidgeted audibly in his seat, causing the cracked leather to complain. Afterwards, he tossed the cigarette on the dash. He had bitten his fingernails down to the nubs now and, with nothing solid left to chew, was going for his cuticle. Tiny flecks of blood had been left on the cigarette from where he had handled it with his raw fingertips.

"It has to be him. There's no other way."

Melancon studied his young charge out of the corner of his eye. Tomás had called Felix twice more since they had left the Seventeenth Ward. Felix's girl-friend, Tina, had also called once, to say that Tomás had called, and to say that she was worried about Felix and about the young boy. The phone was driving him mad, and at the same time he seemed unwilling or unable to turn the thing off. As a result, Detective Herbert was looking like he might be folding under the pressure.

"Pull it together, kid. You're talking like you've already made up your mind about things, and that's a dangerous place to be. You go looking for easy answers and you end up grabbing at straws. Day one stuff. You're better than that. Pressure is just part of the job. Don't let it get to you. You put everything else aside except for finding Andre. This is all going to work out."

He heard Felix blowing out a deep breath from the passenger side. It sounded almost like the car had taken a nail in one of its tires.

"You think Melph knows where the kid is?"

"No, I don't believe so, Felix. I think if he knew it we would know it, one way or the other."

They were getting into the outskirts east of the city now—a place where the ground was sodden and took a disdain for man's buildings. A place where levees failed and graffiti lined the concrete and tired-looking men pushed tiny lawn mowers that would never be able to fight back the sedge. Indian grass and swaying palmetto fronds reached up from empty fields next to buildings in various states of decay. Kudzu vines and high-water marks covered the few soldiers who had withstood the swamp's voracity. Even the roadway itself lifted up, taking a federal aversion towards the local soil, as if to say that it wanted nothing to do with this untrustworthy native ground. The view, on the other hand, was quite excellent. They could see the city behind them clearly through the crisp blue air, a bastion of constrained life among all of this water waiting to one day gain reentry. In front of them, the endless tops of trees, broken only by the top of a defunct amusement park, its painted spires and twisting metal breaking the tree line in a jarring interruption.

As the roadway went higher and the detectives burned further eastward, they were more and more confronted with that iconic view that anyone leaving the city in that direction was bound to notice. It was always a surprising thing, seeing it there where it clearly had no right to be. The broken tops of toppling roller coasters. A Ferris wheel with its cars all hanging loose and rusty. The sign that somehow still read "Closed for Storm" fifteen-odd years later. From their elevated position, they could see all of these things and more—crumbling spires, broken slides, a parking lot broken up by the roots of small saplings and cypress knees. Big pools of water filled up the low spots where manicured green spaces were supposed to have been. A merry-go-round, near the center of the place, had a collapsed roof, exposing the faded horses and mystical creatures within. It was a lingering reminder of the past, of the great storm, and it haunted the east side of the city still.

"How much do you reckon they spent building that amusement park?" Felix asked. "And it shut down, what, the first week? Millions and millions of dollars just gone. Poof. And they've never been able to do anything with it."

"They can't do anything. They should have never

built a theme park in a swamp to begin with. That, my young friend, is nothing but a monument to foolishness. To the limits placed on us by geography. Gives me the creeps every time I drive by. I hope it rots back into the swamp sooner rather than later."

They passed the old amusement park and got off on a side road that wound its way down to the shores of Lake Pontchartrain. Here the roads were a mere suggestion, more potholes than pavement, everything all washed out and clinging to stolen earth. The El Camino struggled to make its way. Finally, the two detectives pulled up at a complex of buildings a stone's throw from the shores of the lake itself. Though Melancon couldn't quite make out the waters beyond the high earthen levee, he knew it was right there. He could smell it, that smell like your dog had come home salty after swimming in the sea all day, and he could almost taste it on the air, too. A wooden, brackish taste on a moist wind. They left the car and walked towards the doors.

How many had smelled and tasted this breeze as their last sampling of freedom for a long while, he wondered, before they tagged you with the crazy stick and you lost everything.

The main building was out of date, not much medical about its wide antebellum porch with its Doric columns and slate roof. Maybe they had converted it.

Or maybe it was the whole point, Melancon thought. When someone led you here, someone you trusted, they didn't want you getting any hint of what lay inside, waiting for you. At least, not before they could get a few burly orderlies flanking you. No, all they wanted was for you to get some wind off the lake, look up at an old plantation building, follow them inside and—

He shuddered.

It wasn't so bad in reality as it was in his mind, though. At least not what he saw of the lobby, where the place seemed almost a decent sort—quiet, clean, clinical. But this was only the lobby, after all. Where were the padded rooms? The electroshock therapy, the—

"Can I help you gentlemen?"

He found himself at the front desk, a young woman in a white uniform greeting him and his partner.

"Yes. We're here to see Lashawn Jones."

"Oh." The young woman blushed a bit. "She has asked...she's not taking visitors."

"By her own request? Or doctor's orders?"

The receptionist scratched her head, fiddled with some paperwork in front of her. She put her hand on a phone receiver, but she didn't pick it up. Then she looked at the detectives with clear hesitation.

"Are you journalists?"

"No, no," Melancon said. "This is very important. We're private detectives."

He put his credentials down on the counter. "But we're not here to cause any trouble. We're here to help."

She leaned forward and ran her eyes over the impotent badge.

"She's in a very vulnerable state right now, gentlemen. She has had a bit of what you might call a breakdown. She doesn't want to talk to any policemen, I assume that would include the private sort as well."

Felix slid his raw hands onto the counter and leaned into the woman, flashing her a smile.

"Do one thing for us. If it doesn't work, we'll go on our way."

"And what's that, young man?"

"Tell her we're here about Louis Armstrong."

Soon after, they found themselves sitting at a foldout table and watching a large woman being led into the visiting room. She was unrestrained, tall and formidable in stature, wearing a gown of sorts, and just on the verge of being overweight. She looked still young, still pretty around the face—but motherly in a stern sort of way. Her latent beauty was clearly marred by terror and loss, both of which showed themselves in an expressive scowl on her face. Her stricken eyes bounced between the two detectives, and she began muttering to herself as she sat down, adjusted her too-small chair and looked up at them expectantly.

"Who are you?" she asked, still wearing the scowl —though it was softening now into a pouty frown.

"We're here about Andre," Melancon started.

She sniffled, her eyes wincing and mouth crinkling with hidden pain. "I figured out that much. The damned nurses here won't tell me a thing. I ask and I ask. I want to see the paper, watch the news. I want to call him. But they just stuff pills down my throat. I thought...I thought someone was supposed to listen. I thought that was what this was all about. I can't sleep but can't stay awake either. You ever feel anything like that?"

The two detectives looked at each other.

"Is Andre okay?" she said, her voice cracking with the sound of oncoming tears.

"He's—" Felix began.

"He's fine." Melancon cut the young detective off, shooting him a pregnant look. "As fine as he can be, under the circumstances." He gave the woman across the table a contrite smile, but he could read the suspicion plainly in her face.

"We were just wondering what you might be able to tell us about the boy, seeing as how you must have been so close. We're told that Andre will only talk to close family members. That's adding a lot of difficulty to the investigation, seeing as the boy is the main witness," Felix went on. "You raised him up, didn't you?"

Her eyes creased and she tucked in her lips. Melancon pulled a tissue from a box on a nearby table and passed it to her. She took one and pressed it to a leaking eye.

"Little Andre. Little Andre. Little hayseed. You never seen a boy like that. Never." Her gaze fixed to a far wall, where she stared for some time. When she snapped out of her haze, her eyes lost their fuzziness and again became small and angry. She turned on Melancon and snapped at him.

"How you know...about Louis Armstrong? You're the police?"

The old detective put out two hands in a gesture of placation. "We're friends. Friends of Andre's. Friends of Mr. de Valencia, his tutor. Mr. de Valencia is a wealthy man who harbors a great love for your son."

"Stepson."

"Right. As I was saying. A friend of Mr. de Valencia's is a friend of ours. He has great respect for Andre, and this situation has him worried sick. Sick about Andre's future."

"I'm so damn sick of hearing about that boy's future. Mercy. You'd almost think some folks ain't alive and living and breathing the way they love to carry on and on about the future. Say, what's it matter about the future when you going to take a bullet in broad daylight while just doing your job, Detective? And I'm the crazy one?"

She clenched her jaw and rapped her knuckles on the fake wooden table a few times, looking down at it.

"Well, what is he like, then? Right now. What kind of boy is he?" Melancon asked. "It's hard to tell when he's as quiet as he is."

"He's a daddy's boy. *Was*...a daddy's boy. Mostly talked to his daddy," she said. "He never would listen to me, even though I been his mama for damn near ten years. But he never acted up either. He really didn't need to listen too well, because he mostly just did right all by himself. A grown little boy, kind of. Just not much good at...you know...the *social things*. He couldn't go to school. Couldn't make friends with the other boys. Oh, he talked to me sometimes. Mostly when he was upset. But he almost never got upset. Only thing he ever fussed about was his music and his horn. He's just quiet, you know. There ain't nothing... you know...really wrong with him. In fact, he's real smart."

Melancon nodded, trying to imagine raising a silent, headstrong genius. He nearly shuddered at the thought.

"Well, we aren't here to upset you...but the boy...

he needs his family. Now we understand he was released into the custody of your...brother Melph."

Her sniffling stopped. "Melph?" she asked.

"That's right. We thought that you had—"

"Yeah...I had told the police to give Andre to Melph. Is that where he is now? At Melph's place?"

The two detectives shot another wary glance at one another.

"Melph was in the...in the war, you know? I'm not sure which one. Someplace real hot. He came back and just wasn't the same. He's got some problems from all that. Some of that...shell shock what you call it. I don't know if he can take care of Andre, long-term you know. I've got to...try and get out of here somehow before..."

They eagerly waited, each of them gripping their seats, to find out before what exactly. But Mrs. Jones seemed to pick that moment to change track.

"We had a fight, you know. Me and Andre's father. Me and Renato. It was about Andre. I don't know why I'm telling you this, but we've been having trouble. Trouble with money. Well, actually that's not quite right. We've been seeing the trouble with money coming for a long time. I don't work, you see, because I have...well, I suppose I don't need to tell you, because you can see me sitting here. I have always had some issues, with going outside. I do it, mind, but I get worked up when I have to do it a lot. So I mostly stay in. Then the roof started leaking last year, the hot water heater broke, and Renato started worrying the city might lay some people off with the tourist season being smaller than usual. So we...we had a fight...about Andre. It was a fight we've had a few times before."

"So what was the fight about?" Melancon asked, as carefully as he could.

She sighed, looked around the room. "At least you listen. You're the first man in a suit that has listened to me since this whole thing started. Even if that suit looks like it belongs in the seventies. You don't have a wife, do you, Mr....? What did you say your name was?"

"You can call me David. And you are right, no wife, and never had much of a sense of style either. I find both can distract a man from his work, from his purpose."

She looked at him for a long while, clearly trying to draw out some meaning from the tired-looking old man. They made eye contact and she wasn't the first to avert her eyes.

"David...we fought for the same reason all married couples fight. Money and children. You know...I suppose you must know, if you're friends with Andre's tutor...and about Louis Armstrong...I guess you must know plenty about Andre's talent."

"His horn blowing. Yes, we do," Felix said.

"Well, Renato was very...well, he didn't want

Andre getting a lot of special attention. Not yet. It was very important to him that Andre had a normal childhood. He didn't want Andre being drug around from this show to that show, doing concerts, getting on TV and all that. Not yet. He said that he thought it would ruin the child, particularly with how shy and quiet he was, to be pushed out in front of crowds like some kind of trained seal or something. So, he was very, very protective about that. Meanwhile, I was getting phone calls from that Julian Oliver...offering us five thousand dollars here, ten thousand dollars there...and once even twenty thousand...for Andre to give concerts, be on TV shows, and so on and so forth. But it was always a big, fat NO from Mr. Adai, from Renato. Like to drive me crazy. See, Andre is Renato's only son, and when they come down here from Greensburg—"

"Whoa, slow down now. You mean Andre and his daddy...aren't from New Orleans?"

"Well, depends on what you call *being from* somewhere. Andre wouldn't even remember the place, most likely. He's been right here since he was three years old. That's when they left Greensburg and came down. Ten years ago. I met Renato the first weekend he was down here, can you believe that?"

Melancon had his notepad out now and was furiously scribbling. "Sounds like fate," he said when the tip of his pencil broke.

She nodded. "That's just what it was."

"So, Andre wasn't born here? But in Greensburg. Which is..."

Felix had it pulled up on his phone and extended the map over towards his partner's field of view. "About an hour and a half north of here. Small town. Not far from Amite, actually."

"Up by the Mississippi state line?" Melancon asked.

She nodded again. "No, sir, Renato was definitely not from the Seventeenth Ward. He was an old country boy, even though he hid it pretty well. One of the first things that made me notice him was the way he walked down the street all slow, like he still might step on a snake, or like he was looking for a place to fish."

She almost smiled, but that smile quickly turned downwards into a grimace. "Maybe he wasn't cut out for this place...this place with all its guns and blood."

Melancon was doing his best to keep her attention dialed in, to keep the wellspring of information flowing as long as he could. "What about Andre's...biological mom. When did she pass away?"

"She, uhh...well, all I know is Renato always said she went missing from a truck stop. They got those places up there for the long-haul truckers when they come off the interstate, right near the parish line. Casinos with showers and beds. You know the kind of stuff that goes on there? Because I don't, and don't want to either. All I know is from the couple of times Renato talked to me about it. Maybe three or four times over a decade. He wasn't near as quiet as Andre, but he wasn't a big talker either. Not about things like that, anyway."

Melancon scratched his chin, ran a handkerchief over his forehead.

"She disappeared, huh?"

Lashawn shrugged. "I don't know much about it except that when they came down here, she wasn't with them. And I was too happy with my new man to look a gift horse in the mouth too much."

An orderly had walked up behind her and bent down to whisper in her ear. She nodded sadly.

"It's time for group therapy. I've got to get going."

"Do you think...," Felix began, leaving the question unfinished. Her eyes widened and her eyebrows raised.

"You want to know if I'm really crazy or not, don't you?"

Felix reddened, but he slid his hands forward on the table towards her. "We care about Andre. He needs you."

"All I know is...if you can act normal a week after your husband gets shot in the face...you the crazy one. I'm going to do my best, for Andre, but..."

A tear ran down her cheek just then. She turned her head and looked at Melancon a long time.

"If you really care about Andre, there's one thing you could do for me. For him, really."

"Anything," the old detective said.

She dug around in the pockets of her scrub pants and pulled out a folded envelope. The corners were dog-eared, and it looked as though someone had spilled water on it. She bit her lip, looked down at it for a while, and then stuck it out towards Melancon.

"This is from Andre's daddy. It's a letter to him. He told me...if anything were to ever happen, I needed to give this to his little boy. I couldn't do it that first night. I couldn't do anything. But I stuck it in my bag once I knew I was going here. Can you promise me you'll give it to Andre when you see him?"

Melancon could feel the lump forming in his throat. He knew he better not hesitate.

"You have our word," Felix said.

They watched her being led away by the orderly through the double doors of the ward. As they were standing up, Melancon's phone began to buzz from his shirt pocket. He replaced it with the crumpled letter and flipped it open.

"Hey, Janine."

"A hotelier called in with Renato's RTA badge. Says some kid tried to use it as a fake ID. The NOPD has already gone in and taken the card, but I don't think anybody brought the clerk in for questioning. Just thought you guys could maybe...you know...I thought maybe it was a good lead to help you find Andre. The guy didn't let Andre stay, so I guess that means he's sleeping on the street. I don't want to think about that...don't want it on my conscience."

"We're on it," he said and nodded to Felix.

SIXTEEN

I look down at the green, dirty water of the Mississippi. I know it comes from far away and sweeps right through here, and that if I let it sweep me with it, there's no telling where I'll end up or what might happen to me.

But then again, that's already the spot I'm in, isn't it? River or not, wet or dry, free or in some kind of a cage or waif's home—there's really no knowing what happens next. I never thought about it like that, not before this moment peeking down into the swirly river, but suddenly that dark water doesn't seem nearly so bad as a lot of other things that may be coming.

Like this man. He works for a riverboat, stands twice my height, and he knows my name well. "Mr. Adai," he calls out to me, his arms out at his sides like he might lose his balance at any moment. The other passengers are starting to watch now. I see a woman in a sun hat cover her mouth and grab her little son up real close to her. The sense is that I'm *wanted*, just like in one of those old cowboy movies. My picture, my face, is up on the wall of the little cabin overlooking the deck, I'm sure. And then this man comes out, like the sheriff, and now he's facing me down. After he takes another step forward, I feel the energy of his boot thumping down on the metal deck, closer now. I feel I can hear his breathing, even over the music (because the band keeps right on playing) and over the engine. I get that he's proud and nervous and I can smell his aftershave mixed in with that wet-dog breeze coming off the factories and plants near the shore.

I look down again at that water. So much of it. So dark and coming from so many places. But it all ends up right here.

I'm not going to go with him. I won't live with Melph. I know he doesn't want me. Mama Jones probably wants me, but I don't know if she could stand to see me every day wearing Daddy's face and being so quiet, never making friends, just reminding her of everything. She has her own things, just like me. Her own problems. And I'm not going to go and live in some orphanage, either. I'm just not. The Waif's Home for Boys was torn down a long time ago, just dust now, might as well be a fairy tale—torn all down to the ground just like Storyville, just like every place around. Just like everything in this flooded old place.

I'm going to just go on and on, all by my lonesome, until the vanishing point takes me up somewhere down at the end of all this. I still have this choice.

So, I put my foot up on the railing and start to raise myself over it.

"Hey!" I hear called behind me. It sounds so weak and sad, like a voice that has already given up to some horrible but certain thing. That last second on the ledge, I can hear even more feet rushing towards me. At least more people will know, I think. They're coming now in a stampede—so many feet. I wonder if the boat will tip over to one side when all the people gather over here to look and watch what happens to a poor boy like me.

Louis Armstrong was here, before me. He walked on the deck of a boat just like this. Though it might have been wood and not metal. The people would have been different, too. The river water has changed a million times since then, but it's still the same river. He would jump, too. If Daddy were here, he would jump.

I have to do it. I let go of the railing a few seconds before the riverboat man gets to me.

The next thing I feel is like being in space. There's nothing underneath me except the water rushing up quick. The wind tears at my backpack but I keep it on, tight around me as I can, until finally I hit. When I land, it's right on my left shoulder. I know I'm supposed to turn myself into a knife, to cut the water like a high diver, but I land all crooked like a dead fish instead and it hurts something fierce.

Then I'm lost with that pain for a minute in a brown swirl of bubbles. I take a big mouthful of water and my nose fills up with a burning, swampy smell. My head pops up, but the current is so strong. I'm thrashing around, trying to pull in the air, and being tugged away.

My head goes back underwater. I try and close my eyes. I try and think about Louis Armstrong. Maybe this is where the vanishing point will take me. I'll be a part of history and a part of the river forever. Only no books will be written and there will never be a postage stamp with my face on it.

But I don't fall asleep. Not yet. From underwater, I hear one of the loudest sounds I've ever heard. It has a rhythm to it as well, sounding like steady cannonballs hitting the surface. Maybe, I think, this is the music of death. But it isn't. It's the red paddle wheel of the steamer getting closer and closer. It is sucking the water towards itself, stronger than even the Mississippi, and with that water it's also sucking me. I'm being pulled closer and closer towards it, the belly-flopping paddleboards getting louder and—

At the last moment, the wheel grinds to a halt, and the boat passes me by. I'm drifting along in the silty water. Sometimes it sucks me under for just a bit, but never more than I can stand. Otherwise it lets me back up again to breathe every ten seconds or so. Big logs drift by, large pieces of lumber and trash. The river is taking me where it wants me. I stop trying to fight it and give up.

But the backpack is weighing me down. I've got two pieces of metal strapped to me, I realize, in between breaths. A gun and a horn—two pieces of metal and they both want nothing more than to fall to the bottom of this river and rest there for a few hundred years. If they take me with them, it makes no difference.

But some miracle happens. Some spirit watches over me. I don't really know how exactly I get so lucky but I suddenly just open my eyes and I can see rocks only a few feet away. I'm breathless and tired as I've ever been, but the rocks are so close. I start to paddle towards them, but I'm not much of a swimmer, so it takes me a lot of time and energy to move a few feet. When I try to grab for one of the rocks, it's slippery and sharp. When I finally get a hold of one, I can feel how strong the river wants to keep me. For a second I think about just letting go, letting myself be washed down or drowned or whatever else it is that the river wants, because I'm tired of fighting against it, tired of everything, so much stronger than me, pulling me this way and that and having to fight against it. I don't want to run or fight anymore.

But I don't let go. I get the rock in both hands and

pull. Finally, a few seconds later, I'm standing on a grassy bank. I cough and sputter and wheeze and the ground underneath me spins a little bit. Water is dripping off of me and the wind is cold. I climb to the top of the levee and make it over to the other side. Then I look up.

All around me are tombstones, dead trees, but I don't see a church or any people. There's garbage blowing in the wind, the smell of old beer, kudzu vines swirling like the eddies in the river. No cars and no loud music, but the glow of distant headlights maybe a mile away. The sun is getting real low now, almost gone. The only thing here in front of me is just rows and rows of the stones, all of them about the same shape and size, equally spaced and probably neat and tidy once upon a time. Now they're rotting uneven like bad teeth. Some of them have the names of the dead on them, some are so worn as to say nothing at all, some are toppled over and lying flat on the silt. There are a few spots of green grass, a few tussling tops of live oaks with their bushy leaves that never fall off.

I squish forward, realize I'm still only wearing one shoe and that the shoe is waterlogged and nasty. I take it off and toss it away. My feet are cold but the ground feels kind of good underneath them, and it's nice not to have that squishy shoe weighing me down anymore.

I finish coughing up water and I try and shake myself off a bit. The wetness is making me shiver, and

I'm starting to feel pins and needles working their way up into my legs. I walk around a bit to get my blood flowing and look to find a spot that's maybe sheltered from the wind. It's also getting dark. I find a brick wall and crouch behind it, shaking so hard among all those dead people. I wonder if any of them can see me. I take off my backpack and dump it out on the ground and—

My horn.

My horn is gone.

I look around in a panic, but it's too dark now. Hopeless. I turn the bag upside down and the gun falls out, all on its lonesome. It twinkles, all wet, in the dead grass, and that horrible lightweight emptiness is all that's left in my backpack.

Empty air.

I try to think about Louis Armstrong, but I can't even do that. His face, the sound of his beautiful high C, the sweat he wipes away from his forehead as he smiles into the camera in Technicolor—all of those things are gone from me. They must all be sinking down with my horn into the bottom of the Mississippi, which is deeper than anyone could ever imagine. It might as well go all the way to the center of the earth. I see my horn falling to a place where no man can go that is so deep and dark and terrible that you can't even imagine it.

It must have fallen out, it must be gone, it must be sinking still, second by second, into the murky water.

The only thing that's still here is the gun, dripping wet but still all in one piece.

The gun is the only thing left.

The gun and me.

I put it back in my bag and run, no direction, no idea where I'm going. I just want to be away from all of the dead people before they convince me that I'm better off with them. Before they can welcome me. Before they can reach out and—

I come to some kind of an empty parking lot. Everywhere it is broken bottles, discarded underwear, plastic bags. And then I see it.

There, off to one side, is a billboard. A strange place for one, and it looks like it has been sitting here through all weather for years and years. It's faded, torn in the corners, and in the last red glow of the sunset I can see it turn all orange and bright before the sun dips into the vanishing point and leaves me in the dead darkness.

"JAZZLAND: OPENING THIS SUMMER," it reads in large bold letters. "4 Miles North on the 510, exit 182," it says, slightly smaller, just underneath.

And just under that...it is *him*.

Daddy always said it wasn't good to be superstitious, or to rely too much on signs. But that way of thinking didn't do him much good, did it? Not in the end. Maybe Daddy wasn't right about everything. This has got to be one of those moments. Why else would it be here, staring me in the face, right as I'm about to freeze? Right in my darkest moment. It is here, he is here. Just right when I lose my horn and wash up choking near a field of countless dead people.

Louis. He's everywhere in this town. At the center of everything.

And now he's right there in front of me, larger than life, as always. His face must be ten feet tall. Louis, faded and worn and torn by the wind, is still himself. He has one of those faces that you can never miss. It pops out in this dead place. Mr. Armstrong. No mistaking him, not for one second. No one else can blow his horn. No one else can go on, year after year, putting everything happy and right into the world while all of the broken glass and condom wrappers and cigarette butts just float around him.

Above Louis are the tops of roller coasters, a merry-go-round, a Ferris wheel. Behind him are a happy, laughing family. The dad's head has been torn off by the wind, but I can imagine his smiling, happy face as he leads his family into Jazzland for a day of fun together, at Louis's recommendation.

I stare at this sign for a long, long time. Thinking it all over—everything that has happened. My whole life. I don't have a voice and now I don't even have a horn anymore.

All I have is a wet gun, cold bones, and four miles to walk before I can find that final vanishing point.

Finally, it's full dark, and I can't see the sign anymore. That's okay. I look right past it. I look right down the road. I know that's where it has to all end. I know that there's only one way I can be happy. But there's one thing I want to make sure of.

I take the brass shell casings out of the pocket of the army jacket and toss them on the ground, right in front of the sign. I hope maybe the police will find them here, will take them in and put them under a microscope. I hope they will find out if these are the bullets that—

But then again, it doesn't matter too much. You can't change the past, and there's no sense in trying. All you can do is try to just leave a little trace of yourself and hope that maybe someone will care.

Louis is still just there smiling, even though I can hardly see him in all the darkness.

For the first time in a long while, the hurting stops, and I smile back.

SEVENTEEN

"So, the kid comes in here, and he's what, thirteen? You take his father's ID badge and you turn him back towards the street? That what kind of a man you are?"

Felix had an accusatory finger pointed in the hotelier's face. Melancon had to use two hands on his partner's shoulders to pull him back to a safe distance.

"What do you want me to do? Urchins coming in here all the time. I reported the stolen ID, which is all the NOPD wants me to do. Who are you? You're not even police officers. Why don't you get the fuck out of my hotel before I call the real cops and—"

"Alright, look," Melancon said, two hands of supplication raised as he took a step towards the hotelier, putting himself bodily between Felix and the tired-looking man. "We're hunting that missing boy. He has a family that cares about him. I'm not sure if the cops told you, but that badge belonged to his recently murdered father."

The hotelier cut his eyes to the side, rocked on his little stool a bit.

"Are you watching the game while I'm trying to talk to you?"

The man shrugged, but he didn't return his attention. His eyes were indeed cast in the glow of some out-of-sight television. Melancon could even see a ball reflected in motion across in the man's glasses.

Felix stepped around Melancon and slapped an angry palm down on the counter. "You. Tell me everything, every detail about the boy. How was he dressed? Did he say anything? Where do you think he was going?"

Melancon realized what a fruitless effort it was, how pointless this interrogation was bound to be, but he felt his phone buzzing in his pocket before he could alter this impotent line of questioning.

Janine again.

"Hey, Janine, we're talking to the hotelier right now. Guy won't—"

She cut him off.

"Andre went in the river, David."

"What?"

Melancon didn't want to believe it. He shot his young partner a panicked glance. Felix caught the gist of it right away, turned away from the surly hotelier.

"Get down to the Chalmette Battlefield. It happened right near here. There's a search-and-rescue operation. But you know, David...I mean, I don't have to tell you...about the Mississippi River...in March."

Her voice was cracking. Whether it was sobs or a bad connection, he couldn't be sure. He could hear men yelling urgently in the background, the sound of a chopper starting.

"What do you mean, 'he went in the river'?" Melancon asked, not wanting to simply unpack those straightforward words himself. This odd question caused even the impassive hotelier to look away from his television, but only for the briefest of moments.

"Just get down here, David. I need you," she said and hung up.

They were back in the El Camino in twenty seconds, the chassis of the thing fishtailing a bit as Melancon gunned it out onto Tulane Avenue.

"Did she say what happened? Do you think he's dead? Drowned?"

"She didn't say anything, kid. Just that he went in the drink. We're about to find out, though. Hold on."

Melancon made a few quick turns, taking them down shorter side roads, the car flopping over the deep potholes.

"Felix."

They took a quick turn onto St. Peter. Both of them had to grip the handles as the car squealed against the moist asphalt and righted itself straight again.

"This is not the quickest way, partner," Felix was saying, "You need to take 10 East or Rampart to—"

"Felix!"

"What?"

"Look behind us."

"Holy shit, is that—?"

"I think it is."

What Melancon saw in his rearview was disturbing to say the least, given the already tense circumstances. The dark green Explorer was now inches away from the El Camino's bumper—the same Explorer they had seen park in front of the house on Leonidas Street just a few hours earlier, driven by a long Marine sniper who had stepped out onto the St. Augustine and somehow avoided wetting his feet in that street-wide puddle. But the windshield of the Explorer was just a little too tinted to be certain, a little too dark to see the face behind the wheel.

But Melancon knew.

"It has to be Melph. He's been behind us for the last three turns," the old detective said, followed by a stream of expletives. He was adjusting the rearview mirror and dodging potholes as best he could as he got them onto Basin Street, flying past the detective agency and onto the eastbound highway.

"Lose him," Felix said, drumming his fingers nervously on the dash.

Melancon pressed his foot down on the gas pedal, merging into heavy late-afternoon traffic and weaving between three slower-moving cars, quickly breaking out into the fast lane. The old engine complained in a dull roar, the metal pinging and thumping with the exertion.

"I don't know how much of this the old girl has in her," Melancon yelled, gripping the steering wheel tight in both hands.

"He's still there!" Felix cried.

"Hold on."

Up ahead there was an exit blocked off by an accident of some kind—three or four men standing around a series of orange cones, a tow truck, and a broken-down vehicle.

Melancon waited until the last moment, and then pulled the wheel to the right, knocking one of the cones down and passing within inches of the back of the tow truck. On the exit ramp he lost control of the vehicle—the old El Camino spun around once, banged up against the guardrail, and righted itself with clear road ahead and no trailing enemy behind.

"We lost him," Melancon said, nearly breathless. "You alright?"

"Yeah, good job," Felix replied, gripping the dashboard with both hands. His face had gone ghostly white. "Are we still mobile, or we need to get out and push?"

Melancon gently caressed the gas with his loafer and was relieved when the car moved forward again.

When they had made it a few blocks, Felix slumped in his seat and finally released his vise grip on the dashboard. "I hate to say I told you so, old man, but I told you so."

Melancon nodded, pulling onto the two-lane highway that would take them to the battlefield.

"Maybe you were right. I don't know why he would be following us if he's an innocent man. Or maybe he thinks we know where Andre is and is hoping to gain some glory by finding the kid at the same time as we do."

Felix shook his head. "The kid he lost? Anyway, I don't have a good feeling about anyone finding that boy now."

As they pulled into the battlefield tourist parking lot, the situation indeed appeared far from hopeful. Dozens of police cruisers were there, some of them flashing their lights. A small tent had been set up in one corner of the grass, where a few uniformed men stood around a table, their map fluttering in the late-evening breeze. The moon had come up over the river, casting a beautiful though grim light down on the whole operation. Rescue boats were moving around in the current, and in the distance, the detectives could see the bridge lit up and twinkling as commuters made their way home to the West Bank.

Felix's phone rang.

"Tomás, we're doing the best we can. It would be helpful if you stopped calling me every—"

The young detective's mouth swung open. "Hold on, I want Melancon to hear this." He pressed the speaker feature on his device, letting Tomás de Valencia's voice enter the vehicle.

"I heard a...a sound. I thought, someone could be breaking in downstairs. It turned out to be only the wind. But in my fright, I went for the *pistola* your father, Felix, always kept in his desk drawer. The one in his office, you know, with the pearl handle. You remember, of course? But I was shocked to discover that...the gun...it is no longer there. And I thought to myself, who has been in the house? There has been no new cleaning woman, no new anyone...except..."

Melancon slapped his fedora down on the dashboard, rubbed his forehead in exasperation.

"The kid...but why would he?"

"Shit," Melancon said and stepped out of the vehicle.

He found Janine standing on the banks of the Mississippi, right near the old veteran's cemetery that flanked the eastern end of the battlefield. She was watching a few Harbor Police boats churn through the muddy water near the shore. The big beams on the front of the boats danced across the surface of the water.

The old man tucked his hat under his arm. Lowering his head, he made his approach.

"Damn," he said, low and solemn, as if it were some kind of a prayer. "Damn it all."

Janine turned to face him. "We don't know yet, David. Not for sure. It isn't over until we find him. If we ever do. All we know is that a security officer on board made a positive ID on Andre. Scar on his neck and all. He phoned it in to the police on shore but then foolishly tried to apprehend the boy himself. When he did, Andre jumped overboard and was last seen going under the water."

Felix showed up, still pale as a ghost. Paler, perhaps. He mouthed some silent words to his partner and shook his head. "This is..."

But his words failed him. Taking a running start, the young detective kicked a piece of driftwood so hard it splintered into three pieces. It must have hurt, from the look on his face afterwards. He stalked off into the darkness, cursing under his breath.

Melancon peered down at the swiftly moving murk, wine-colored and final, the wakes of the rescue boats troubling its man-made shore of rocks and clay. After a long life on the banks of this capricious river, he knew it well: knew precisely what that fickle and violent water was capable of—it took zero mercy on those who disrespected it.

"You reckon Andre was a good swimmer?" the old detective asked.

Janine's eyes went soft and warm and full of a shimmering wetness, but she gave no reply. Melancon put an arm around her, a bold move considering the many professional eyes surrounding them, but she leaned into it anyway.

"We fucked up," she said, sniffling a bit. "All of us fucked this right up. The boy paid the price."

Melancon held her there, but the moment didn't last long. Just as quickly as she had fallen into despair, Janine straightened her back and wiped her eyes dry. Now she was again a stalwart police detective, surveying riparian operations.

"Andre has...or had a pistol. We think," he told her.

"Why would he—"

"We don't know. Protection, maybe? Just thought you should know."

"I guess it doesn't matter too much now," she said, looking out at the river.

"We'll take a look around," Melancon said. "Try to stay out of y'all's way as best we can."

She nodded, looking away from him and out towards the boats, a painful quiver to her lip that perhaps only he could detect.

Melancon wound his way through the uniforms, shook a few hands, until he finally found a place alone in the darkness, where he wiped away a bit of moisture from his own eyes. Tired calf muscles took him up on the earthen levee, where he could look back upriver and see the twinkling downtown buildings blocking out the stars. Between him and the central business district, he also spied the old sugar mill looking craggy and angular in the night. It was not a place he was particularly fond of, since recent memories from that decrepit old monument of industry were unpleasant to say the least. They were recollections of a cruelty that, when brooded on in the slightest, sent a long, slow chill up his spine. There was just something about this part of town —something that attracted dark happenings. But it wasn't just this part of town. It was the whole place. The world entire, as it would, kept on being cruel.

There's a chance he made it to the shore, David Melancon told himself, though he wasn't quite sure he could really believe it. The river was so broad, so strong, so deep, and Andre so small and helpless. But it wasn't over until it was over. He had to push those thoughts away and bring his whole mind to bear on the search.

"Felix!" he called out. He could see the young detective's flashlight waving against the rocks up ahead.

"Yeah, I'm over here. I've got something!"

Melancon hurried down with some speed, nearly falling face-first after the corner of a large stone caught his loafer at a compromising angle. But he reached the muddy, lapping shore below the earthwork and looked down at what his partner had found.

His heart quivered. This forlorn thing. This stomach-churning sight.

A strange brass fish. How it shone in the flashlight's heartless beam.

A horn.

The horn.

His horn.

Melancon put his hand over his mouth and barely held back a sob before it could announce itself.

Felix was shaking his head, still muttering something under his breath. He picked up the instrument carefully, reverently. With a cringe he tilted it downwards, letting the accumulated river water trickle out of the fat end and down onto the rocks.

"Do you...pray much these days, partner?" the young detective asked.

Melancon didn't answer. He couldn't. "Keep looking," he choked out. "I don't have a light."

As Felix made widening circles around the find with his beam, Melancon tilted the horn this way and that, looking at it closely. The twisted tubes. The three valves. The flange of bent metal. All of it looked duller and more used upon closer inspection.

Or maybe it was just the way it took on the moonlight.

What a thing, he thought to himself.

"Here!" Felix shouted from the other side of the levee.

In the veterans' graveyard, fifty feet from the river, Felix had found a waterlogged shoe, just the size a thirteen-year-old boy like Andre would wear. He held it up in triumph.

"It's a miracle," Felix was already saying, casting his eyes and his torch around for the boy, as if he might appear behind a leaning headstone at any moment.

Melancon felt the shoe. Yes, it was wet. The water was cold and dripping, and there had been no rain for several days. There was no other possible explanation.

"He has to be alive. It's too far from the river, Felix. He's alive, damnit. He's alive!"

The two men embraced for a moment, laughing and nearly jumping with excitement. Melancon shook the horn above his head before finally restraining himself and straightening his fedora.

"Should we tell Janine?"

"Not yet, Felix. Keep looking."

"I don't see the other shoe anywhere."

They kept the search up, casting out in random directions, yelling the boy's name and getting no response. Then they came into a dark unused parking lot filled with trash and broken bottles. Just as

Melancon was beginning to doubt himself, just as he was beginning to wonder why a wet shoe had given him so much hope, he spied the billboard.

"It's Satchmo," Melancon said when Felix's flashlight lit up the ripped and tattered sign announcing Jazzland, Louis Armstrong prominently featured in the center of it all.

Felix ran towards the sign. Halfway there he stepped on something lying in the parking lot, which sent him sprawling. He fell onto his back, gave out a small yelp and rolled a bit, holding his ankle. A metallic tinkling followed the yelp as something rolled out into the darkness.

"Shhh...I twisted it—"

"Felix, look what you tripped on."

Melancon picked up Felix's dropped flashlight and then, with his handkerchief, the metal objects that were lying next to it.

"It's all brass tonight, I guess. Shell casings from a high-powered rifle. Maybe a 30-06."

Felix stood up slowly and brushed himself off.

"What does it mean?"

"Andre must have left them here."

"Could just be some redneck shooting off rounds."

"I don't know, Felix; we aren't in the middle of the woods here. A high-powered rifle this close to civilization would probably be reported. These are just sitting here, right near the sign of you know who. And look."

He held one up in the beam of the flashlight.

"It's shiny. Like it has been in someone's pocket and not sitting out here in the weather."

"You think he was trying to tell us something?"

"Not trying," Melancon said, pointing at the portrait of Satchmo blowing his horn, "doing."

"You think he's headed to Jazzland? To accomplish what?"

Their eyes met then.

"Felix. Why would he be going to an abandoned theme park dedicated to his idol, late at night, with a pistol but no horn, by himself, after he'd already attempted something like suicide a few hours ago? Having left behind some important bit of evidence lying in the middle of a parking lot?"

Felix started to answer but seemed to choke on the words.

"Do we tell Janine?"

"No, we don't want anything to spook him. We go in quiet. And we go in a hurry."

"I don't think he would—"

"I don't know, Felix. Wouldn't you be thinking that same way if you were in his shoes? I mean, you're rich and loved and I'm sure you've thought about it a million times. Now imagine how he feels, dripping and cold with river water, walking off into the night, hunted, with no one that loves him around and able enough to take him in."

"I just...alright, let's go quick. It would have taken him an hour to walk there and that's about how long it's been since his little swim, right?"

"We walk right through the detectives and don't say a word, partner. Keep it off your face. We have to get there fast before..."

He couldn't finish the thought. Instead, he started walking.

EIGHTEEN

Melph Jones stared out of the cracked windshield of his Explorer. He was an old hand at staring, watching, waiting. There was a certain rhythm to it, a cadence of mind so easy to slip into. It was almost like a meditation of sorts. He could watch for hours—the mechanics of patience were a thing the Marines had taught him well. When death and dismemberment were on the table, when hate and anger were in full flare, it was often the more patient man who won out. Common sense to apply that stillness to this fucked-up situation, which also called for him to be slow, deliberate, thoughtful. There was an edge, and he was teetering on it to be sure.

So, he was practicing that patience now from a parking spot in the pitch-dark shade of a gnarly oak tree, right at the edge of the old battlefield. But it wasn't an easy vigil.

First: the lights down by the river. There were so many that it was like some sort of a military operation down there. He watched thick beams dance across the dark water, and it all gave him a tightness in the chest. That frantic, urgent scanning of the river by so many men—it could only mean one thing. But it was a story that Melph Jones couldn't yet tell himself. He would have to sit and wait to be told it by someone else, before he could ever truly accept it. Or maybe see with his own eyes what the search would dredge up and drag onto the shore. No, he wouldn't create such a thing out of thin air. He would wait for it to be real— hours, days, weeks of patient, silent waiting if need be.

Second: he was the superstitious type, no matter what he told himself. He did not like a battlefield, particularly not one as old as this and flanked by the acid-eaten stones of countless war dead. He'd known too many living soldiers. He'd eaten with them, slept alongside them, shared bottles with them, and then watched them die, watched them wiped away, mere smudges of humanity. He didn't have to come to a place like this to see and remember them. Their faces and names and ways lived in his head, always, and there was no comfort to be found here among their remains.

Thankfully, he didn't have to wait long for a new development to take him away.

The old El Camino was already pulling out,

retreating, making the long loop that cut through the historic grass, headed away from the search operation's brilliant glow. But why? Why were those two detectives fleeing from all of this hullaballoo? Surely this was the center of things. Why were they headed back out onto the highway, away from all of the flashing lights and boats and—

Melph slipped his ride into gear and crept forward, headlights off. Radio silence.

Where were they going?

He'd lost the detectives earlier, but it had been easy to pick up their trail again. The authorities always traveled in packs, and you'd never catch them dealing with trouble alone. He'd seen the chopper flying low just minutes after losing them, and had simply followed it as it went cutting across the night sky. From there he had soon fallen into the stream of police cars headed east.

But he hadn't even needed to do all that. Not really.

Because, after all, the two detectives had Andre's phone.

And the detectives were smart, but not too smart— just smart enough to maybe find Andre, if he were still among the living, without being smart enough to realize how easy it was to track the location of a family member's cell phone.

The problem was that it was *so easy*, Melph knew

he wouldn't be the only one with the Find My Phone application open right now.

And therein lay trouble number three: somewhere, nearby perhaps, he knew there was another set of patient, vigilant eyes watching the little dot float across the map. That, more than anything, gave the waiting an edge.

He crept forward a little more quickly now, keeping to the right where the shadows of the oak trees lay across the asphalt. The detectives were nearing the highway. Melph let them pull out and get well ahead this time, but he would not let them get away.

Because they knew something.

About Andre.

They had to. Why else would they be leaving now? They had to be getting close. Whatever business those two were about would lead him to the boy, he was sure of it. And he had to get there before—

Melph was nearly T-boned pulling out onto the highway, preoccupied with his hunt. The pickup truck swerved and let out a few angry honks before righting itself.

He had to focus. No mistakes.

The detectives took a left on Highway 47 and headed north, away from the river. He followed them at a distance, keeping his headlights off and using the app to make sure he was going the right direction. The El Camino entered a long stretch of road that cut through empty grassland and began picking up speed. He let them go, continued northward.

Several miles he burned through the darkness, past canals and old defunct drive-ins and dive bars. He lit a cigarette and took in the scenery.

Mostly nothing but alligators out here, big nutria rat made toxic from all the human runoff. This is where you were likely to find a dead body rolled up in a carpet, though, Melph thought. He kept waiting for the detectives to pull over by some fetid pool, to shine a light out onto his nephew's bloated corpse floating nearby. But they never did.

Instead, they pulled into a turnoff. A dead end.

What was this place? There was something oddly familiar about it.

Melph rolled onto the shoulder of the highway and, from a distance of about two hundred yards, peered through his binoculars. Hard to make out much, except what he could discern in the El Camino's headlights. As he looked, it became clear that the two detectives had turned into the entryway of a large abandoned parking lot. A parking lot to what exactly? He couldn't be sure. There was nothing much out here, or so Melph thought, having spent almost his entire life on the opposite end of the city. He could see the older detective had stepped out and was running his hand across an iron bar that stretched across the pavement, barring access. Melph killed his engine and waited in the darkness for what might happen next.

The detective was back at the wheel now, and the El Camino revved a few times, bouncing forward. It pulled off to the side and stopped with its headlights pointed out into the muddy darkness. Finally, the tires squealed, the chassis fishtailed, and the old car charged headlong into that wetness, forging its own path towards the parking lot.

Brave. Brave but stupid. Did that thing even have four-wheel drive?

They must be in some kind of awful hurry, and that had meaning.

Melph started his engine and crept closer, until he could see the clumps of mud being flung out into the roadway. The El Camino's headlights moved forward bit by bit until they gradually became nothing but a glow off in the deep swamp.

But this wasn't the only glow now. In the darkness a new set of lights had emerged. They appeared on the deserted stretch of highway, coming from the other direction. Melph couldn't make out the type of car, but he had a pretty good idea. Whatever and whoever it was pulled off the road and into the darkness before he could size it up and confirm. He waited and listened for the slamming of a car door. When he heard it, he reached immediately into his back seat and prepared himself.

Fucked-up situation was putting it lightly. And he had known so many.

Here was the leather case in his lap now. The one tool for situations too far gone to repair. Melph pulled out the long object from inside of it—metal and wood and more metal. Inscribed on the stock was a stag's head. On top was a long-range precision scope. He gripped it in his hands and found his breath growing still, his thoughts calming, the mechanics of patience all revisiting him in the darkness of this swampy spot.

He opened the door and stepped out, rifle slung over his back, and charged into that darkness.

NINETEEN

I'm walking through the big park. There are rusty metal beams overhead, broken beer bottles everywhere, the smell of swampy water blowing in the cold wind.

It only took me an hour to get here. I'm getting good at running. But now I'm here and there's no more running left to do. I have to be brave.

I go through a series of fences. I don't know why I keep going, but maybe it's because I'm not ready to do it yet. One place is as good as any, I suppose, but still, I walk a little further.

I climb over a low cinder block wall, and halfway down I suddenly hear a sound that makes me freeze.

Claws on metal. Scraping, crawling, ticking against a hollow piece of tin. I feel so terrified, and I wonder why. Didn't I come here to die? Whatever it is making that awful sound, it can't do anything worse than just kill me. Still, I turn in a panic with my breath sucked right out of me.

But it's just a raccoon scurrying across the top of the busted merry-go-round. The little creature comes out into the moonlight and looks down at me with his beady black eyes. But I don't have any food, so he loses interest and goes on about his evening. It's quiet again after that. Except for the few crickets and frogs that have come out a bit too early for spring, it's nice and quiet. Quiet for what I've come here to do.

People like to think places like this are haunted, or spooky, or filled with danger in some kind of way. But they are wrong. It's the *people* who are really dangerous. That's why abandoned places like this are the safest places in the world. It's the city back behind me that's dangerous and spooky. It's the places that are filled with men and women that you should be afraid of.

The quiet is good, I suppose. I guess maybe some music would be nice, music to make me brave. Because I'm so scared, tired, cold. But I still don't stop walking. I still don't just do it. Because...

Then I see him. Of course he would be here. Of course it makes sense that I would come, just like the poster welcomed me to.

In the moonlight, you can hardly make out his face. He is quiet, still, frozen forever in plastic. From a pedestal, he is watching over everything, the lonely king of a wet kingdom, and I know him in the darkness from the way he's standing—holding court over lily pads and kudzu creepers. Crawfish make little mud chimneys at his feet, but there's no mistaking the silhouette of what he holds in his outstretched arms, the joyful curve of his cheeks.

I feel peace. Here, in this lonely and abandoned park, maybe I can finally have some sort of a choice about what's going to happen to me. Everything here has been drowned a hundred times over, left to sink, but Louis hasn't yet been brought low. Isn't that a sign? To find him standing here in the middle of the swamp?

I'm thankful for that, in these last moments. I know, in my heart, about how he's just a plastic copy of someone long dead, someone who never knew my name, or that I would even exist. But it doesn't matter. He's something important, perfect even, and I'm not. My eyes are adjusting now and I can see him more clearly. Louis's face is smiling, happy, his eyes are wide and friendly. The paint has faded and some kind of a moss has covered his forehead.

It's going to happen one way or another. The vanishing point is at the end of every single road. It's there for everyone. I can tough it out and try to go through life as an orphan without a voice, without even a horn to make a sound with, but after all of it I would still just end up right here. And maybe I couldn't even have my own choice about it. Even Louis Armstrong died. When he died, he was in his seventies and a hero across the world. His voice floated out into space and he was on the cover of *Life* magazine, but he died all the same. That was a long time ago. I'm thinking about this and I'm realizing that not only am I an orphan, I'm also a crazy person. A crazy orphan who's too shit scared to even speak. A crazy orphan who let his daddy die and now is just sitting here in the middle of the night, in an abandoned place, thinking about a man so long dead and—

Anyway, I'm glad Louis hasn't fallen apart yet, so he can be here with me. That way I won't be alone when I do it. Or, at least I won't feel like it.

I pull the gun out of my backpack, look at it for a long time. I like the way it shines in the moonlight, almost reminds me of my horn, which I know must be settled down now onto the bottom of the Mississippi by now. The pistol is heavy and the grip on it looks like it's about worn out, like it has been gripped a lot of times by sweaty hands, just like my horn. I wonder for a second if it has ever been fired in anger. I wonder about every place it has been and all of the things that led it to being right here, in my hand.

I think about my daddy and wonder where did they bury him.

I put the barrel of the gun up to my temple, feel the cold ring of it against my skin. I hum an old song in my head to try and make myself brave.

Oh, when the saints go marching in.

Because that's the way that everything will happen. Something wonderful will bloom and then it will fall away and die and rot and maybe flow away with the river.

Oh, when the moon turns red with blood.

It's all coming to the vanishing point. I can see everything that could have been and won't ever be.

Oh, when the sun refused to shine.

Will it hurt? Not so much as living will.

Oh, when the trumpet sounds its call.

I pull back the hammer, like I've seen them do in the movies. I put my finger on the trigger and start to squeeze.

And I think about Louis Armstrong.

TWENTY

"You couldn't have brought two flashlights, Felix?" Melancon said, nearly falling over a crumpled steel trash can. It rolled off into the darkness with a thud. The truth was, it wasn't the darkness but the cold. A chill had worked its way into the detective's old knees and turned his legs clumsy and stiff.

"Sorry, I didn't know we'd be creeping around an old abandoned amusement park tonight," Felix replied. "This was never in the help wanted ad. You hold the torch, then, man. I've got to lug this horn anyway. Thing is heavier than it looks."

It wasn't only the cold either. Something else was causing the old detective to stumble and shake: the empty, forlorn feeling evoked by the failed park. The boarded-up popcorn stands. The wind sweeping the torn, wet flags. It was all working overtime in Melancon's imagination. It might have been closed to the public, but the dark thoughts had an all-access pass in this place—no waiting in line and free concessions for life, step right up, all you nightmares and demons.

"I don't see any sign of the kid," he finally said, after the next three twists and turns revealed nothing but more decrepit carnival rides.

Felix said nothing but kept marching forward, and the two of them penetrating further into the rusty labyrinth of iron and cement.

Melancon, flashlight in hand, was now fully able to take in the place. It was with grim curiosity that he explored his surroundings, and he couldn't help but find the defunct optimism of the place absolutely chilling. It was like looking through the photo album of a young, ambitious person who died tragically the night of her graduation. It was like looking at a picture of Julie Melancon. The rides never ridden. The happy little statues peeling and rotting in forsaken mires like half-baked goblins. The painted murals all covered up in graffiti and black mold. All of this wasted potential hit the old man right in his gut with some unspeakable reckoning, a haymaker of regret.

"He's got to be here, right?" Felix said, skirting around a gaping hole in the pavement. "Or are we crazy?"

"He's got to be here," Melancon repeated.

"I'd say either he's here or we're crazy," Felix said. "Only two things that make sense to me."

"Only two things that make sense."

The further in they went, the more the hair on the back of his neck stood at attention. The park was far from silent. From around every corner and collapsed roof came strange metallic patter. The two detectives pressed forward nervously, sensitive to every rustle of leaf and dripping of condensation. Further on, they came to a burgeoning forest of small saplings that had broken through the cracked cement. They wove through it, next circumnavigating a hot dog stand turned island, its craggy wooden corpse surrounded by a frog-filled pond. Past that, they entered a maze of fences and pillars supporting some large skeletal attraction, built to dizzying heights overhead, so high that the flashlight barely reached its upper vertebrae.

They then came to a clearing bathed in moonlight, some unrealized focal point of the park.

And there he was—standing in full view, under a large statue.

"Andre!" Felix shouted.

But Melancon had already seen. There was the boy, withered since the old detective had last set eyes on him. The child cowered, shielding his eyes with one hand and wincing as the high-lumen beam hit him.

And what was that? The thing the boy held in his hand? Bile rose up in Melancon's stomach and he froze as he recognized the terrible shape of it, the glint, the horrible direction it was pointed. He put a hand up to still his young partner's advance towards the boy.

"What do you have in your hand, Andre?" Melancon said, unable to hide a quivering weakness in his voice.

"We're here to help you," Felix cried.

"He's got the gun," Melancon whispered to Felix, though it needn't have been mentioned. It was clear enough what they had walked in on.

Andre backed away from them slowly, ducking behind the statue and peering out at them, the pistol still pressed firmly to his own temple.

Melancon tried to soften his voice a bit, lowered the flashlight out of Andre's eyes and walked forward as casually as he could, a great fear hidden and heavy in his chest. "Whoa, there, young man. Where are you going? Don't do anything just yet, not until we get a chance to talk to you. That's all we want, just to talk. Okay?"

Andre continued to peek at them from behind the base of the pedestal of the statue but did not show himself or step back out into the clearing. Melancon, his mind doused suddenly with adrenaline, happened to glance up and see who it was depicted there in faded plastic.

"Oh, hey. Man, you just can't get away from Mr. Armstrong in this town, can you? I see you found your friend, Louis, right where he's supposed to be. That's lucky."

The boy looked up at the towering figure above him. There was wetness on his cheeks, puffiness around the eyes, a dour angle to his mouth. Andre lowered the pistol from his temple but did not let go of it.

"Andre, your daddy, he was..."

The boy raised the pistol again to his head, a deflated look in his eyes.

Melancon thought for a minute, glancing up again at the statue. "What I meant to say was..."

A silence lingered while he chose his next words carefully.

"You know...about Louis Armstrong...he's not here anymore. He died...and, yeah, it was a tragedy. But if he was here, I think he would be really, really proud of you."

Andre stared off into the darkness behind Melancon, a million miles away, before returning his gaze to the old detective. The boy tucked in his lower lip and again lowered the pistol.

"What are you doing?" Felix whispered.

"Just trust me on this, Felix. I have a hunch," he whispered back.

"You're not a fucking psychologist, partner. You don't know what you are doing."

"Well, unless you see any PhDs around here, I'm

going to try my best if you don't mind. I don't exactly have time to get a twelve-year degree at the moment."

"You could make things worse. What if he...?" Melancon could hear the defeat in Felix's sigh, deep discomfort in the sharp intake of breath. "Alright," he finally said. Melancon put a hand on Felix's shoulder, cleared his throat and picked his words with all the strategic intuition his near seven decades could muster.

"If Louis were here, Andre, he would tell you that you have a great gift. He would tell you that...well... that you are a marvel of creation."

Where this all came from, Melancon couldn't have explained in another seventy years, but it flowed out of him nonetheless, one syllable after another.

"And a gift like the one you have...that isn't something that you can just...take out of the world anytime you see fit. Because that would be selfish, you see. What you've got is an important thing, a thing you have to protect, to not be selfish with. I think Louis Armstrong knew that about you, and he wanted to protect you and your gift from the world. And he might have even...died because of that. Because that's the thing about being gifted...a lot of people want to take your gift and use it for themselves. Now that Louis is gone, there's nobody here to protect you. That means you have to be a grown-up all of a sudden... means that you have to protect your own gift from all those that want to take it from you. That's tough and I know it."

The boy actually nodded. It was slight, but it was there. As his scowl began to fade, Andre took a cautious step out into the clearing, towards the detectives. The pistol hung limply at his side. Melancon pressed on now with renewed confidence.

"Hell, I'll bet Louis, if he were here right now...in the flesh, I mean, no disrespect to the statue...but I bet he wouldn't blame you one bit for thinking of doing what you're thinking of doing. He probably knew some tough living in his day. He was a great man, in the end, though, because he stuck it out. But the secret, Andre, is that tough living makes you tough in turn...and so I think old Satchmo would also tell you not to act rash, to think about all the joy and beauty and happiness a person like yourself could bring to the world once they survive one of the worst things that can happen to a person... I mean, Louis kept right on going, right? He liked to sing about how wonderful the world was, now didn't he? Now can you imagine the world without Louis Armstrong ever having existed? Imagine the world if he had shot himself in some dingy park at thirteen...I don't know about you, but that wouldn't be a world I would want to live in. Louis would tell you, if he were here, about the awesome life you're going to have playing music for people and making them happy."

Melancon turned his head towards Felix, whose heavy eyes were staring right into him with a confused look of hope. The old man cracked a sad smile, glanced down at the horn in Felix's hand, nodded it towards Andre.

The young detective timidly held out the brass so that Andre could see it. "Think this belongs to you... and I think that piece in your hand might belong to me...trade ya?"

A look of absolute joy came over the boy's face, louder than any words. Andre leaned forward, towards the horn, and it seemed he might even reach for it. But he stopped short, wincing out of a pained resolve.

"Look, there's something else," Melancon went on. "Felix and I...we went to see your stepmama. She gave us something for you. It's from...well, it's important anyway. You're going to want to read this letter one day, son."

The boy gave a meek nod, wiping a tear away from his eye. The gun still hung loosely at his side. Melancon took the damp envelope from his coat pocket and handed it to his young partner.

Now Felix was inching his way towards the boy, an envelope in one hand and the horn in the other.

"Come on now, kid. There's a lot left for you here."

Andre took a step forward. He let the gun drop from his hand, where it rattled down on the pavement, then took the horn from Felix. Next he grabbed the letter and sat down cross-legged with the two items in his lap. Melancon approached him cautiously, kicking the pistol out into the damp darkness and finally putting a fatherly hand on the boy's sobbing shoulder.

"It's going to be alright, kid."

Felix flanked the boy, putting a hand on the other shoulder. "I know how you feel, Andre," he said. "I really do."

They sat there for a minute, just letting him cry. The set jaw, the narrow-eyed readiness to die, the white knuckles locked on the butt of a weapon—all of that had completely dissolved. All that was left was a boy who was deeply hurt. And he sobbed like a small boy in the thrall of deep, silent pain. He cried until he dampened the coat of the old detective even more than the swampy romp through the park had done, clutching a brass horn and a crumpled letter.

Until, all at once, he stopped crying.

He grew very quiet and began to stare out into the darkness with a focused, unwavering gaze. So intently did he fix his sights that both detectives couldn't help but follow his eyes.

"What are you looking at, Andre?" Felix asked.

"She's here," the boy said.

Melancon covered his mouth with his hand, shone his flashlight out into the darkness, saw nothing.

"You can speak," Melancon said, joy filling his voice. For a second, the content of what Andre had said, the words he had spoken, didn't register. Nothing mattered so much as the simple, melodious sound of his voice, still the high-pitched and unbroken soprano of a child.

But Andre did not mark this moment with any special acknowledgment or weight, nor did he say more. Instead, he raised a finger and pointed urgently out into the darkness. Melancon, with his hand still on the boy's shoulder, felt a sudden tightening that he couldn't yet comprehend.

"Howdy," said a female voice, causing Melancon and Felix both to jump.

Felix let out a small cry of surprise and splayed his hands out under himself lest he topple over. The voice had come from just behind a pillar, and it was terribly close. So close that Melancon couldn't imagine how they had been snuck up on in such a way. He felt the waves of adrenaline, which had only just begun to fade, return with a vengeance.

Melancon turned his flashlight on the voice instinctively, revealing, in the orange glow, the shape of a woman. Whoever she was, she must have been extremely practiced at sneaking. She had gotten the drop on them completely and absolutely.

It was then he noticed what she was holding.

"If you don't mind, that light is a bit hard on the eyes," she said, chambering a shell into the shotgun to make certain she got her point across.

"Now stand back from the boy," she commanded, in a voice that invited no argument.

But the detectives could not comply, even had they wanted to. Andre stood brazen, unmoving between the detectives and the tip of that scattergun, his arms spread wide—one hand holding his trumpet and the other still grasping the crumpled letter.

She was dressed well, too well for the dank and dirty place, for sneaking and slinking around old abandoned places such as this. A plain green dress, unsullied and well-fitting, hung with its hem just down to cover the top of a pair of heavy leather work boots like a man working construction might wear. She wasn't some squatter, living here in filthy isolation. Who, then? Melancon tried to trace a connection, taking her in with all the clarity that only sudden danger can bring. She was pretty, middle-aged, curvy but stern-faced and even a bit menacing around the eyebrows. Of course, the shotgun didn't help. A deep-red wine-colored lipstick was smeared across her full lips.

Melancon felt his hand start to itch, to pull towards the revolver on his belt. But the woman had him completely dead to rights, so he stilled his fighting instinct and simply raised his palms high above his head, quietly cursing himself for his failures and inattention.

"Come here, baby," the woman said to Andre. She had a singsong twang with gravel around its edges.

"No," the boy replied.

Her eyes narrowed but the shotgun barrel sank a few inches, pointed now in the general direction of Melancon and company's guts, poised to rearrange their insides with a simple twitch of her index finger.

"You've always had a memory on you, Andre. So smart, but you just look back at me like I'm a stranger. I wonder why that is. Maybe you just decided you'd go on and forget. Or maybe you're just pretending. Pretending even to yourself, maybe. But I think you're too smart not to know. Too smart not to know I'd be coming to get my baby. Ain't that a fact?"

Andre shook his head.

"Let me help you remember, Andre."

The boy again shook his head.

"Oh Lord...I..."

She paused, looking closely at him, took a deep breath and piped up with a high melody.

"I want...to be...in that number," she sang.

Andre's mouth opened; he took a step forward. He dropped his horn on the cracked cement, where it landed with a cymbal crash.

"Oh when the saints...go...marching....in."

Andre took another step towards her. The woman rounded out her song with a soft, soulful flourish—the gravel in her had all disappeared and what was left was a choir-leading church voice.

"Mama?" Andre said.

"You got it."

The two stared at each other for a long time.

"Come on, baby. We're going home. We're going where the grass grows, leave all of this noise and commotion behind. At least for a while. There ain't nothing so bad a little time in God's country can't solve."

Andre nodded. "Mama...," he said.

"Still got that scar on your neck...just like me," she said, pointing to a thin line that marred her well-kept skin along her jugular. "We're survivors, Andre. You and me. We don't need anybody else. And when you get ready to blow your horn, we're going to be big. Your name up in lights, and me right there watching over you. Now how that sound?"

Andre's brow had furrowed. He looked lost, confused, but he steadily crept towards the woman, searching her with his eyes.

"But first, I think we need to take care of your two friends here," she said, hoisting the shotgun. "See, Andre...that's the thing about city folks. They don't know how to leave well enough alone. They don't have enough meaning in their lives...they step around home-less people and what mess is in their own front yard, but they sure enough want to check up on whatever it is you're doing yourself. Now, every time I step out onto my porch, do I want to be worried about them? About someone hunting me? Or trying to take you away? No, indeed. No, indeed. So, what I want you to do is this...walk over there, Andre. Take your horn with you and cover your eyes. Put your mouth to the mouth-piece and blow it as loud and as long as you—"

Andre shook his head, wiping fat tears away from his cheeks with the sleeve of the army jacket. "No, Mama. No," he said.

"It's going to be alright, baby, just wait over—"

A shot rang out in the darkness. Melancon winced, his whole life flashing before his eyes. He was certain the shotgun, pointed right at his belly, must have gone off. The ringing in his ears, the weakness of his knees, the memories and impressions of a long life rolling like a film reel behind his tightly closed eyes—surely he was in the lobby of the offices of certain death. Surely his final appointment had only just arrived.

But no, he could still feel his heart beating, though it had definitely skipped a beat or two. His guts still churned with inference, hunger, sorrow and despera-tion. His head, bald and haranguing as it was, was still attached to his body and in one piece.

A yelling had started—a desperate, pained, mournful wail. Was it coming from his own throat as he numbly went through his death throes? No: the yelling was coming from the woman.

The hem of her dress was wet now with blood, and her knees buckled as she sank to the cement. One of her hands remained on the shotgun, but the other worried her thigh. Melancon could now see the bone poking through the dress, the blood spouting forth in a great deluge of red.

Melancon regained himself as quickly as he was able and, seizing the moment, he grabbed both young people and yanked them into the darkness.

"Run," he whispered, in between ten-gallon gasps of wet winter air.

That was what they did, the three of them sprinting down the root-broke pathways and past the attractions covered with kudzu, with more gunfire erupting at their backs as they went, hurrying them along through muck and frog puddles and shattered glass. The water splashed around their knees as they took no more pains to avoid it, unseen creatures slithering and leaping away from the three fugitives as they went.

Melancon did his best to lead them, but he wasn't as quick as he had once been. Those cold, brittle knees made for hard going, and the two young men were soon far ahead, leaving him to follow as best he could. A few hundred yards into their mad dash, he found himself out of breath, doubled over with stomach pain. Luckily, he spotted Felix and Andre just ahead and darting into the open doorway of an abandoned building. He followed them into the blackness of concrete boulders and beer cans.

He found them inside behind a pile of trash, near

the remnants of an old campfire. "That's your mother?" he stammered, still unable to believe what he'd witnessed.

Andre slowly nodded.

His hand was now free to draw his pistol, and Melancon crouched by the doorway, listening to more bullets fly just outside. It sounded like a battlefield.

"Who's shooting?" Felix asked. "They aren't shooting at us, are they?"

"I don't know, Felix. Just keep your head down. Keep an eye on Andre. Also, dial Janine," Melancon said, suddenly clear-headed in the safety of the concrete room. He tossed his old flip phone at Felix, who barely managed to catch it in the darkness. "Tell her to get the NOPD out here, choppers with searchlights, the works."

"Got it."

As soon as Felix had delivered the message, Andre reached out and took the phone from his hand.

"Is this Janine? I'm ready to talk. I'll talk as much as you want," he said into the receiver.

TWENTY-ONE

From up in the NOPD helicopter, Jazzland looked to Janine like one of the children's toys pediatricians keep in their lobbies. Twisted loop-the-loops and colorful scaffold stuck up above miles of dark, wooden swamp-land—all of it cast in the city's dramatic glow.

It was her first time hovering above this particular patch of earth, but she'd heard plenty about it, mostly in the form of bellyaching over the years from the salty patrolmen unlucky enough to find themselves on Jazz-land duty. Rousting the teenage lovers, dare-maddened college kids, and occasional squatters was not a popular amusement among the officers. But while she hadn't been to the *park* before, she'd been in this figu-rative position more than a few times now, and it was starting to wear a bit thin.

Somehow, regardless of how intensely she stonewalled him, it was always David Melancon that was standing at the center of her cases when the rubber hit the road. Her feelings for him, and their hot-and-cold history over the years, made his central involvement in all this complicated. Or was it vice versa? She admired him, but she also deeply disapproved of the way he went about things. It was an old way, too casual and reckless. It got results, but it left a lot of loose ends in the process—and she'd spend weeks afterwards retying all of those knots while he just bathed in the glory and "forgot" to fill out any paperwork. She would have admitted a small bit of envy over the way his gut always seemed to lead him to the right place. What she resented was the chore she always had of bailing him out when he got himself in far too deep, as she was preparing to do right at this moment.

They had begun to descend now, the wings bending the tops of the trees.

She pointed to the pilot. "Up there, on the coaster rail. Can you see him?"

When they got low enough, the figure of a human clinging to one dizzying rung was unmistakable. A man. She could even see his T-shirt billowing under the pressure of the chopper blades. When the spotlight hit him directly, he rolled over. It was then that the three of them—Janine, pilot, and an extra officer—could see that the man had a long rifle.

The man shielded his eyes with his free hand.

Then, with an acrobatic bend of his lanky torso, he was gone. Janine caught just a flash of him shimmying down some support beam and then didn't see him again. The officer behind her was already nervously yelling into his radio about an armed and dangerous suspect. The flashing lights of the police cars below showed that the ground cavalry had also arrived, and there was a mass of blue-blinking strobes swirling in a frenzy around the entryway. Though they couldn't seem to access the parking lot, she could already make out a few uniformed officers walking into the park with long beams of light jerking suspiciously out in front of them.

The chopper circled, its spotlight shining down into a central square in the park. It hesitated there on some large figure and, seeing at last that it was nothing but a harmless statue, swung back out into the swamp again. Still no man with the long rifle.

Then, under the boughs of a great oak, he appeared. But he wasn't firing or running or engaging the officers in a Mexican standoff, and he had taken no hostage. Instead, he was walking with his hands above his head towards the officers, the rifle nowhere to be seen.

"We got the son of a bitch," the officer yelled over the whirling blades.

Janine grabbed his radio.

"Suspect appears to be surrendering. I repeat, he

may be turning himself in." She had to yell, getting little but white noise and static back. "Proceed with caution, but he appears unarmed. I repeat, he appears unarmed."

The chopper made an even lower pass, keeping its light trained on the thin figure of the man. He had sunk to his knees now, a tight circle of officers closing around him. All of them were shouting orders, guns drawn and holding back ravenous German shepherds.

"We got him," the radio finally said. "Suspect in custody."

"HE LIKES HOT CHOCOLATE," Melph Jones said to Janine. They sat across from each other in one of those white, joyless rooms filled with cameras.

"Oh, you know what he likes?"

Melph shrugged, rubbed an invisible blemish off the table with his big thumb. "He's here, right? Y'all got him here? He's probably cold and hungry. Give him some goddamn hot chocolate."

She waited. Waiting usually worked best for her. Just give someone enough empty space and eventually they would start filling it. Don't react to bluster or intimidation or stony silence—just wait. Nature hates a vacuum, and so do those under suspicion.

But Melph Jones didn't seem like a textbook type

of case, and maybe he didn't care all that much about vacuums and long, pregnant pauses. Maybe he just wasn't that type. He looked like he'd been through a bit of pressure in his life, and this wasn't anything new. Maybe she was going about it all wrong. Even when he cursed, he did it calmly and with a sly grin on his face.

"You must know you're facing multiple charges."

Melph rubbed his face. "He is here, right? Andre? He's alright?"

She didn't answer his question, but he seemed to read it in her eyes.

"Yeah, he's alright. He get his horn? I saw him drop it."

Janine studied him closely. "You saw that through the scope of your rifle, I guess?"

There was one of those pauses again, lingering and interminable, while the two of them stared at each other.

"Can I get a cigarette?"

"You can't smoke in here. What year do you think it is?"

Melph frowned. "Tell me your name again, honey."

She blew some hot air out of her nose and counted to three.

"Janine. It damn sure ain't honey."

"Right. That was my mama's name. It's a pretty name. I always liked that one."

She lowered her eyes, trying her best to peer into him, to pry the lid off this locked chest. There were so many questions, so many angles of approach.

"I tell you what, Janine-not-honey. You can get me my cigarettes or get me my lawyer, up to you. And another thing—"

He burst through the door just then. There was no knock, and she could hear him rounding off an argument with the officer who was meant to be guarding the entrance. David Melancon, full of piss and vinegar, tossed his fedora down on the table before she could get a word in. He then pulled up a spare seat to the table and straddled it, face-to-face with Melph Jones.

"This is my interrogation, David," she started to say, but her lack of conviction was plain in her voice— she knew the man had the right to be here. At least from a moral standpoint. He'd followed this case since day one, been shot at, and finally produced the result they were all looking for vis-à-vis the safe return of young Andre. Still, if it weren't for his decades on the force and war-forged connections with the old guard, she might have considered this the last straw, had him dragged out of the station and slept soundly over the whole matter. But she didn't. Not yet, at least.

The bastard. The look he gave her, before he turned his full attention on Melph Jones, said he knew what she was thinking.

"Did you save my life?" Melancon asked. At first,

Janine wondered if he was asking her. But that was not the case—the old detective had his bright blue eyes focused solely on the suspect.

Melph shrugged his shoulders and then raised his chin. "You find her yet?" he asked. "Dumb question, right? You wouldn't be here if you'd found her."

Melancon cast a glance at the corner of the room, where a camera blinked back at him. "No, they're looking. But you know...a swamp at midnight isn't a place where you can find much. But we will find her. Trust that. Cigarette?"

"Lord, yes."

Melph was already reaching out a greedy hand, even before Melancon could produce the pack from his coat pocket. But when he saw the brand, Melph stopped short. His hand froze in midreach. The big palm turned upwards and then recoiled. The old detective placed the pack of smokes down in the center of the table, faceup, and crossed his arms.

"B&H?" Melph laughed—a short, breathless exhalation that was over as quickly as it began. Then he turned serious, his jaw hardening and his gaze leveling on David Melancon. "I don't smoke menthol. Thanks, though."

"I didn't think so. But I bet you know someone that does. Now you didn't answer my question, and it wasn't rhetorical. Did you save my life?"

"She snuck right up on you. And you're, what,

supposed to be this tough guy detective? This old soldier? You wouldn't have made it one day in—"

"I'm not supposed to be anything, now answer the question." The two men were leaning into each other.

"Yeah...I suppose...I probably did save your life. She'd have killed you. Not a doubt in my mind. She'd have killed me too. She may have already. They still got the chair at Angola far as I know."

Melancon pulled out a ziplock bag containing two empty rifle shells, put them on the table next to the unopened cigarettes.

"When Janine here has the boys dust these shell casings for prints, whose prints is she going to find? Besides Andre's, I mean. I assume they're the same caliber as the rifle you used tonight. I even assume they were fired from the same gun."

Melph scratched the side of his head and leaned far back in his chair. "Yeah."

"I'm doing a lot of assuming here, but bear with me....can I also assume that these here...that they're the casings from the murder of Renato Adai?"

Melph nodded. "I reckon so."

Melancon slapped his hands down flat on the table. "So, yeah, I'm supposed to be this big detective, but I fail all the time. I failed tonight to protect the people I needed to, and without you I would have died. And right now, I'm having another massive failure. Failure to make heads or tails of you or what your involvement in all this is. I need you to start talking some sense, partner. Because—"

"You can't be that stupid," Melph interrupted.

Melancon got that faraway look in his eyes. "Try me," he said.

TWENTY-TWO

That Janine didn't like it much, but the old yat finally got him some decent cigarettes, let him smoke for a minute and collect his thoughts. Strong, tarry cigarettes. Coffin nails. Cowboy killers.

How magnanimous. Was this the good cop, bad cop type of deal? Whatever it was, it didn't matter much. Melph was here, and he was ready. Just needed a little space to breathe before the big plunge, and now that he'd had it there was nothing else left but to jump in.

"Last summer," Melph began, and could already feel the ears perking. "I met her last summer."

What a summer.

He blew out bitter smoke and recalled, not without fondness, the shape of her body in that tight green dress, walking across the green grass towards him. The swing of her hip was like the crook in the river. Down by the Fly. A hot day. Everybody sweating, cooking food that they were too hot to eat. Ice-cold beer. A football was passed around and someone took it too seriously. A bunch of soldiers with no one to fight but each other. A support group he was part of. Guys that weren't over it yet and might never be, trying to pretend life was normal and fine.

"And there she was," Melph told the eager detectives.

And there she was, striding across the grass and landing, somehow, right next to his unfolded lawn chair. Pretty nails and long lashes and dirty sandals, some rugged loveliness about her. He had assumed she was a friend of one of the guys' wives. Not the right thing to do, to assume, but something about that green dress, something about the twangy talk and the way she ate chicken wings with lipstick on, that had made it easy.

"So, when you met her, you didn't know she was Andre's mother?" Melancon asked.

Melph gave the old yat a cold look. "I'm telling it now. Shut up and listen, damnit." He stubbed his cigarette out in the ashtray, lit another.

She had come on strong. A country girl who, it seemed like, didn't know a thing about big city living, even though (and get this) her name was Nola. Melph loved that—being a tour guide for civilization. It made him feel like he had protected and saved something valuable back in the Marines, and now this was his reward, getting to show it all off. He liked taking her by the hand to lead her to this or that thing, while she stared wide-eyed like it was all the first time. The live oaks, the belting brass, the bright colors on the squashed-together shotguns stretching down the block. She loved to drink, tequila on the rocks and wine and gin, and could usually handle it. She could cook too. That didn't require any civilization. Crawfish and gumbo and red beans and tamales and pecan pie. She was zesty and full of fire, even for a middle-aged woman like that. And in the bedroom, she—

"You aren't answering the question. Answer the question. Did you know who she was?" Janine demanded.

"No, I had no idea who she was, okay? You think I would have fucked with her if I knew she was Renato's ex-wife?"

It was true, he hadn't had the faintest idea. He'd never even really noticed anything strange about her way of disappearing whenever Andre or Renato came around. Maybe she was just taking things slow. Maybe she just wasn't ready. But still, she had her way of getting quickly quiet when their names were mentioned. She refused, secondhand, his sister Lashawn's many invites to come to family dinner. They all wanted to meet the new girlfriend, for her to be a part of things. It was no wonder.

Love will blind you.

"Yes, I said *love*, damnit," he told the gawking detectives, without provocation.

Melancon cocked his head and nodded thoughtfully.

"Love?" he said.

"Love," Melph said.

Some nights they would stay in, lie in bed and drink and listen to playlists Melph would make special for those nights. She liked jazz and blues and hip hop and she would sometimes get so overwhelmed with it that she would stand up and dance by the closed window, the levee train rattling the house as it passed by the river.

Happy times, last summer.

"Then came the fall," Melph said.

One autumn evening, after they had cleaned off two bottles of red wine and were lying in bed listening to music, she'd turned and paused the playlist, asked him suddenly if he trusted her.

There was an awkward silence in the interrogation room for a second. Melph looked down at the long ash that had crawled up his neglected smoke.

"Did you trust her?" Melancon asked.

"I told her I did."

"But did you?"

"Just listen."

What had followed that night was a very long and

very sad story about Nola's past. Melph had heard these types of stories before, but this one was truly black and pitiful. She'd taken a whole third bottle of merlot to tell it and by the end had been weeping and sobbing. In the story, she, as a young and innocent girl from a small town, fell in love with a truly wicked man. The man was the local beau—handsome and charming and well liked. But these virtues and charms didn't survive the first few years of marital life. Their time together soon turned into a cruel and abusive nightmare. He was cold, distant, prone to spells of violence and rage. To make matters worse, she had twice been pregnant, and twice given birth to this man's sons. While she loved the two boys unconditionally, the relationship between man and wife had soon become untenable. One of the boys, the youngest, would pass away at only two years old, further straining everything.

"Andre had a brother?"

Melph raised his eyebrows. "She said that he died, ten years ago. Maybe Andre doesn't remember. I don't know, since the little dude don't say shit."

"How did he die?"

"Nola didn't say and I damn sure didn't ask."

"Go on."

"So anyway, she tells me this long story. She says the man beat her, cut her. She even showed me a scar on her neck where she said that he cut her."

"Same scar as Andre's got?"

"I didn't think of it that way, not at first, anyway. I didn't make that connection. The way she told it, this mean bastard took her son away from her and ran off. Stole him right out from under her and left her alone way out in the sticks."

Telling the story seemed to have taken a toll on Nola. She'd passed out that night in a puddle of her own tears, the wine staining her usually white teeth. But Melph hadn't been able to stop turning the story over in his head. His love, though, had made him stop just short of questioning it, of questioning her. Still, he'd lain wide-eyed in bed for hours after hearing the tale, Nola sleeping her wine-heavy sleep on his numb shoulder.

In the cold light of day, she'd been embarrassed, asked him to forget it, to never repeat what he had heard.

But something had changed in her. She'd gotten a little colder somehow, quit cooking as much, drank less around him and became more reserved. He hadn't seen her for a few days after that. But she came back. They kept seeing each other, all the way through winter and into the new year.

"I have a resolution," she'd said to Melph, as they kissed out on the dance floor at the Maple Leaf bar, "Auld Lang Syne" being sung by a mix of junkies and college kids on a beer-sticky floor. But she wouldn't say what it was.

The first time she'd asked about Andre, the two lovers had been riding in the car towards downtown New Orleans. Somewhere on St. Charles, they had passed Renato driving his streetcar back towards the Seventeenth Ward. Melph had pointed him out, honked his horn, and kept on driving as if nothing special had happened.

"Who is that?" Nola asked.

"Sister's husband," he answered.

"He's got a son, right? A boy?"

"How'd you know that, Nola?"

"The boy. Is he...alright?"

From there, she'd begun to ask about Andre constantly. About his life, who he was, what he was doing. For weeks it went on. She wanted to know every detail about his horn and his silence, his lack of friends, his infatuation with Louis Armstrong, his shrink appointments and the high-brow Hispanic he took lessons from twice a week. At first, Melph had just figured that the girl had a terminal case of the baby rabies. That was why she was interested, surely. He reckoned that it was just her way of dropping hints about their own future progeny, trying to figure out if Melph was the fatherly type or not. She was at about the age where it would soon be too late. That fact, coupled with her sad story about her child being taken away from her—

"I just figured it was the motherhood instinct type of deal. So, I told her all about my little nephew. I didn't think she was being very subtle, but still, I told her every detail. I thought it was weird, but I guess I was also glad she was interested. I was getting to think...well..."

"Well, what?" Melancon asked.

"Stupid. I was stupid. It doesn't matter. What happened next is what happened next. One evening she went out, left her purse. It was lying tipped over on the bed. I went to pick it up and there, inside but come spilling out, was a picture of her. A lot younger, a lot prettier. It was with her and a little tiny boy... a toddler...I thought I recognized...but I couldn't be sure."

He'd fallen asleep trying to understand it, telling himself a lot of little kids looked alike at that age. Still, he'd left the picture out on the bedside table, waiting.

That was when Melph Jones found himself waking up with a wild-eyed Nola straddling him, something cold and sharp pressed just below his Adam's apple.

A dreamy part of him, for a moment, thought she was playing, being kinky. He even tried to grab her around the waist but—

"Don't move," she said. "Don't even blink."

He didn't, remembering the picture again suddenly.

"Look at me."

So, he looked. He saw her completely, as if for the first time. The lipstick she wore, even to bed. The pain in her eyes that maybe he had minimized or wished away for far too long. The way she ground her teeth and the way her hand trembled holding that razor's edge so close into his neck, so close to his jugular vein.

"I see you, Nola," he said. His voice didn't waver or crack.

"Do you?"

"I..."

"I've made up my mind, Melph."

"I don't understand."

"You do, don't you?"

"Shit."

"Melph, listen to me. I'm not going to wait anymore."

"Okay," he said. "What's that got to do with my neck?"

"I'm going to kill him," she said.

"Kill who?"

"Melph, listen to me. Look at me. You can't be that stupid."

"Kill who, Nola?" he repeated. He'd known killers, seen people killed, and he knew, or thought he knew, that she wasn't that type. Was she? But the pain in his neck was not open to questioning. The more she trembled, the more that blade trembled against the thin skin, the only thing keeping his blood where it was supposed to be and not spurting out across the bedroom.

"Did you even listen? When I told you about my ex-husband? Did you even listen, when I told you about my son? He took him, do you understand? He took him and he brought him down here and he has some shit on me that you can never understand, not in a million years. So, I'm here to get my boy back. I'm going to get my boy back the only way I know how. I'm going to get him back and I'm going to help him. We're going to live off of his gift. I'm going to take him places where he won't get to go no other way."

"Woman, I have no idea what the fuck you're talking about," he said, lying completely helpless under the razor. He tried to squirm, but she pressed that edge into him until he could feel a rivulet of blood running down onto his shirt.

Maybe he had known it all along. Maybe he had. *Just smart enough.* Maybe all that patience, all that meditation, all that time spent in circles remembering the thick shit and what it meant, maybe that had done a number on Melph Jones. It was amazing, the way the human mind could block out entire things it just didn't want to see, that protective mechanism kicking in so complete and final.

It had hit him then. But really, he had known it all along. Finally. He looked up at her. The avoidance, the repeated questions about Andre, her sudden appearance at the park that day.

She nodded to him.

"That's right," she said, seeing in his eyes that he knew it, recognized it, embraced it. "Finally."

"What the fuck, Nola?"

"I just want you to know that if you tell them anything about me, when all this dust settles, you'll be digging your own grave. I had to get close to them, without them knowing I was close."

"What are you going to—"

"That's my boy," she said. "Wherever he's going, I'm going there too."

"This whole time?"

"This whole time."

"Really?"

"Yes, you dumb motherfucker. It was the only way, the only way I could get Andre back. You're sweet, and you are good looking. But it ain't about you, Melph, it never was."

"But if he really beat you and cut you, then—"

"Listen to me. The evidence of everything. It's going to be all over. I've got your rifle. I've got your fingerprints on it. On the shells. On other stuff too. I've hid these things from you, Melph. But no one ever has to know."

"But I know. Why do I have to know?"

"You're a part of this now, Melph."

In the tiny white smoke-filled interrogation room, the yat's eyes widened, and he shook his head.

Melph cleared his throat, took a sip of the coffee they had brought him.

"And then she was gone. And it happened before I could... before I could do anything. And that's about the long and the short of it. I tried to clear everything out, everything to do with her. But there was just too much. That's what I was doing when Andre took off. She had left little bread crumb trails all over the place...and there was no way to...well, here I am anyway. That's it."

"Hell of a story, partner," Melancon said.

"You don't believe me," Melph said. "I don't blame you. I wouldn't believe the shit myself except it happened."

Melph pointed to a little nick in his neck. He picked up the B&H cigarettes and let them slap back down on the table, made a dismissive brushing motion at the shells.

Melancon raised his chin. "So, you figured you were going to kill her before she could try to frame you? Or was it more that you wanted to save us out of the kindness of your heart?"

"No. I did what I did for Andre. After it happened, he was my responsibility and I dropped the ball. I tried to go dump some of her stuff in the river. Stuff I thought she might use to frame me. But I didn't get it all. Hell, not even most of it. Signs of her were all over my house. She even painted my door, to my bedroom, that same color as her lipstick. And Andre... well, in the Marines, you never leave a man behind, and I wasn't about to let my little nephew end up with that crazy-ass woman. Especially when he's crazy himself. So, I did what I had to do. I couldn't come to y'all, with my DNA and whatnot on everything."

"And now you just reckon we'll turn you loose?"

"No." Melph shook his head. "Whatever happens to me happens. It's my fault for being so blind."

"Tell us about what happened tonight," Janine said, leaning in.

"Andre's phone," he said, pointing to a bulge in the old detective's coat.

"What?"

"Find My Phone. Ever heard of it, old man? You were carrying around a tracking device the whole time you were out looking for my nephew. I just followed you. I guess Nola got the code or whatever from my phone, did some tracking of her own. Lashawn had installed it on my shit years ago, to help her keep track of where Andre was."

Melancon took the offending item out of his pocket and looked at it, aghast. "Not my finest hour, I suppose," he mumbled to himself as he placed it down on the table near the cigarettes and shell casings.

"So you followed them to the park, then what?" Janine asked.

"This old yat was there, why don't you let him tell it?"

"Because I'd rather hear it from you."

"Well, I climbed up on the coaster with my night scope. I saw her holding you guys at shotgun point. I knew what was fixing to happen. I tried to just wing her, in the leg, like. She started firing that scattergun just blind out into the night. Then she ran off into the swamp. Wherever she is, she's not feeling too good right now. I hope she's dead, I really do. It's better this way, better for Andre. I don't know. If she got away with it, maybe she would have had some legal claim on the boy. Not now, I guess. I don't know what's going to happen to him now, but whatever it is, it's better than being with her."

Melancon stood up, "Let's give the guy a break, Janine. I need to check on the kid."

"What's going to happen to Andre?" Melph Jones asked. "If Lashawn doesn't get any better, what's going to become of him?"

"We don't know, it depends on—" Melancon was cut off by Janine raising a finger as she put her phone to her ear.

"Got it," she said. "Thanks."

"They found her. Dead in the swamp from blood loss."

Melph Jones leaned back and breathed out a long exhalation. He stuck his hands out to Melancon in surrender, ready to be cuffed, looking the old detective dead in his blue eyes.

TWENTY-THREE

Six Months Later

Tomás de Valencia was sitting in one of the finest hotel rooms he had ever been in, carefully tying a bow tie around his neck, when the phone rang.

The official voice on the other end of the line used his full name. Tomás listened to the news as he wheeled himself over to the floor-to-ceiling-window, overlooking a verdant summertime Central Park below.

When he put the receiver back down in its cradle again, a look of pure joy came over his face.

"Boys, boys!" he shouted to the adjoining bedroom. "Let us leave early. Take the scenic route, if you don't mind. I'm nearly ready."

Tomás had never seen a city like this in all his days. He was overwhelmed by the granite and steel of it, like a mountain broken apart and put back together by millions of tireless hands. To be between the buildings was like being in a deep gray valley with no end in either direction. And the people! It was five o'clock, the time of ants marching. The humanity poured forth from every open door, hugging the sidewalks with purpose in their movements, their bodies draped in dark tones and their faces shrouded behind tinted sunglasses. New York City—it smelled like trash and urine and sizzling sidewalks and the spices and herbs of every nation on earth. Crowds were everywhere: underfoot and overhead, coming up from tunnels zigzagging below the earth and down from glinting glass elevators. An exotic place, but thoroughly American, he decided. It was nothing like New Orleans, like a different and opposite pole of the same heavenly body. The speed of things, the hurriedness, the rough edge, and the wealth that made even the Avenue pale in comparison—all of it was enough to make Tomás feel like a grain of sand awash on an inestimably broad beach.

He was pushed by a similarly gawking Felix Herbert, who rubbernecked each wonder of modern architecture as their little trio passed underneath. The boy kept sticking his nose in some antiquated guide book, decades out of date, and using it to pontificate on the many nuances of the skyline.

The old detective, David Melancon, was with them too. He seemed calmer than normal, taking it all in. The man claimed he had been to New York on more than one occasion and reminisced about his honeymoon here, acting as if he was no stranger to the cosmopolitan joys of the place. Tomás had watched the old goat devour plate after plate of sushi just the night before, and it was some spectacle. Though Melancon seemed to be enjoying himself, he certainly didn't blend in in his out-of-fashion clothes. But then, none of them did. They walked (and rolled) the streets with a syrupiness and ease that betrayed them as wholly alien, as tourists.

They had been moving down sidewalks for at least an hour and had nearly arrived. Yet they were early for their engagement. Tomás, spying a pub across the street, suggested that he buy them a drink.

They crowded around a small table in the back. Melancon ordered a club soda, Tomás a scotch on the rocks, and Felix some sort of a beer that was not beer. The room was cool and spacious and had not yet begun to fill with after-work drinkers. It was the perfect place to say to them what had been burning a hole in his chest since the phone had rung an hour earlier.

He cleared his throat, took a sip of the strong liquor.

"Gentlemen, it is such a pleasure to be here with you on this day. We have been through a lot together. And I am happy that it is you who are here with me

284

now, here to be the first to share this joyful news with me. For I have an announcement. And now feels like the time. I'd like to propose a toast," Tomás said, raising his glass and beaming at them warmly.

"What's the big occasion?" Melancon asked, turning his attention away from the window, already lifting his soda in preparation to celebrate the news, whatever it might be.

Tomás flushed. Was it the scotch? The excitement of what he had to share? Perhaps it was just being here now with these two he cared so deeply about. He did his best to retain his composure and dignity, though if he had been able, he might have stood up and danced on the table.

"First, a toast to you two bravest of men, who risked everything so that a young boy could be saved! You are true defenders of the helpless, the downtrodden, the people who need you most. Our city is lucky to have you."

"Aw shucks," Felix said, running a finger around the rim of his pint glass. Melancon took to tearing a bar napkin to bits. But, at Tomás's insistence, the two detectives begrudgingly toasted their own courage.

"Alright, enough of that. Something tells me that's not the big news," Melancon said. "Don't keep us in suspense, pal. Spill it."

"Alright, then," Tomás said, rubbing his hands together as if warming them by a fire. "Just one hour ago, as we were preparing to leave, I received a very important phone call. The paperwork has all been accepted." He paused, waiting as they hung on his words.

"The adoption has gone through!" Tomás finally said.

Felix stood up, a huge smile playing on his face. "It did?"

"It did."

They raised their glasses, higher this time. The few heads in the small pub turned towards them as they raucously yelled and slapped each other on the back.

"You're going to have a son!"

"That's right, Felix. It won't be the first time, but perhaps the first time legally."

"That's amazing. Congratulations."

"What about Lashawn Jones?" Melancon asked when the toasting was done.

"Well, it wouldn't have happened without her blessing. We have talked many times since those dreadful events unfolded. She agreed that this was for the best, though she will still be a part of young Andre's life as she is able."

"And Melph?"

"I heard he was moving away for a while. To Austin. Poor man." Tomás took another sip of his scotch, shook his head thoughtfully as he peered down into the brown liquid, tinkling his ice against his glass. He pondered the strange situation.

"He was lucky," Melancon said. "Lucky and a crack shot. And so were we. Lucky he saved us."

"Yes. Although it was he who saved you that night in the park, it is also fortunate you were able to repay as you did. Who else could have done so much to help the poor man prove his innocence? And to have charges thrown out on the basis of self-defense? Since then, he has put his trust in you, and by extension, in me. He told me as much when I spoke to him recently. And I plan to live up to that trust. If it weren't for him, you fine gentlemen would perhaps not be sitting across from me now. And the news I have just shared may have never come to pass."

"To Melph," Melancon said, raising his glass again. "And congratulations to you, sir. That boy is in good hands. The best hands."

"Speaking of the boy, we must be going!" Tomás said, glancing at his wristwatch and putting his scotch down emphatically. "We wouldn't want to be late."

Outside the streets were busy, but not as packed as they had been. Tomás was a bit fatigued by the exhaust of the many taxicabs, by the noise, by the glass and cement, and by the long journey across Manhattan. But, despite the draining nature of the metropolis, his happiness remained unflagging as they moved towards the final destination.

"A bit more room to breathe now," Melancon said, taking a slow stroll besides his two friends. "Not shoulder to shoulder like rush hour."

"I'm just still surprised that the boy has had such an about-face. Who would have thought, six months ago, that we would be here today?" Tomás said.

"He made his own choice," Melancon replied. "That's the important part. He chose it himself." The old detective lit a clove cigarette as they stopped for a break near a bench.

"It's great the way things turned out, Tomás," Felix was saying, his hands gripping the handles of the old man's wheelchair. "You're going to be a great pop to that boy. I know you were for me."

Tomás put a hand over his shoulder to pat the top of Felix's wrist. "Let's not dally. It is nearly time."

Their destination was a place of great importance. It was an institution that Tomás de Valencia had been hearing about, reading about, seeing in movies and television shows for his entire life. But he had never been there, never once dreamed that, on some wonderous future occasion, he would be sitting in the middle of it. Now it was nearly time. When they turned the corner and saw it, he was slightly under-whelmed, deflated. He cocked his head and wondered, *Is that all?* Near the park, brightly lit with windows all ablaze in the sunset, a plain enough brick building. It did not overwhelm nearly so much as its name did. In fact, it was but a few stories tall and dwarfed by the surrounding commercial enterprises.

They found their tickets at the will call and went inside.

While the plain exterior might have underwhelmed Tomás de Valencia, the inside gave him the lasting impression he had come to expect from a name so world-renowned as Carnegie Hall's.

It hit the old man as he was wheeled to the front, to the handicapped section on the ground floor. The lights were dizzying, the rooftop soared, and multiple balconies overflowed just above him. There was a smell here like an old vault, a mustiness to the place that felt profound and distinguished. Tomás could not help but look up, straining his neck. Finally, here was the grandeur and magnificence he'd been expecting. The audience had not yet quieted down, and the acoustics of the great room doubled the noise of the chattering, which was all focused around the excitement of what was soon to come.

And then the curtain was raised. Tomás could hardly contain his pride, his anticipation. A hush fell over the crowd as the lights dimmed, all except for the main spotlight hitting center stage.

A happy trill filled the auditorium: a quavering, dancing series of notes. The boy stepped into the spotlight, dressed in a suit and tie, fourteen now and wearing a smile from ear to ear. He blew a few more long, doleful bleats, and then leaned into the microphone and took a bow, a gleaming new trumpet in his hands.

"Thank you for coming to see me tonight," he said, his voice cracking with manhood.

And he pressed the horn to his lips again.

For the next hour and a half, accompanied by a band just out of the spotlight, Andre Adai gave a magical performance. Up to dizzying heights and down to blue and wondrous lows, he blew the audacious sounds of a small, faraway place.

It brought Tomás de Valencia to tears, to thrills, to the vague longing for a thing so terribly missed. It was a sentiment, an indulgence so fleeting it might never be captured—a wordless, silent burning that arose from the gut. You either knew about it from feeling it yourself, or you knew it not at all. For that hour and a half, whatever it was, it filled that alien auditorium: wordless, palpable, bombastic. The snarl of love. The howl of want. The bellowing of discontent. The music of the horn was like gold coins twinkling from the gutter, from the eyes of the dead. It was roots breaking cement, empty chairs and high-water marks and all the losing Tomás had done in a long life in which he had finally, at this late hour, realized how much he had truly won.

In the end, when the boy came out for his final

bow to raucous applause, the audience began to stand up.

Only a few patrons stood, at first. The rest soon followed. The clapping was deafening, yet Tomás managed to make his trembling voice heard, at least to the two friends sitting astride him.

"Pick me up."

"What?"

"Pick me up?"

"I don't think—" Felix said.

"Pick me up, damnit."

And so, working together with Melancon, Felix managed to bring the old man to his feet. Tomás, with an arm held over the shoulders of each of them, stood up for the boy and joined the crowd at Carnegie Hall in a standing ovation for one of the greatest sons of New Orleans.

TWENTY-FOUR

When people asked Louis Armstrong why he played the way he did, he said he did it "in the cause of happiness."

For a long time now, I've been thinking about that. About being a soldier for that cause. But I haven't been a very good one, because a soldier is someone who isn't scared. And for so long I've been absolutely terrified. What I've been most scared of is remembering. These days, I practice memory almost as much as I practice trumpet. People like to say to me, *you have your whole life ahead of you*. But people don't say that you also have your whole life *behind you*, moving away from you slowly, like the oak trees on St. Charles getting smaller and smaller as you sit in the backwards conductor chair. That feeling has always made me sick, terrified me even.

But remembering must be done, and after every

performance, that's what I try to do. I put as much happiness as I can into the show. I play for the people and try to give them something beautiful and full of joy. But when the curtain falls, and I've let out all my happy feelings, I've got no more defense. So, I let the past all come flooding back at once.

It is hard, but it's for a good cause. I owe a debt. All the dark thoughts and memories have to be remembered. They have to be unpacked again from whatever corner of my mind I've stuck them in.

So that's what I'm doing right now.

I'm in my dressing room and the after-show jitters are starting to quiet down. I sit on the couch and open the letter. Just like every other time I've opened it for the past six months, an old photograph falls out from between the crease.

I look at the picture and remember.

I look at his round little cheeks, the adorable mess of curly hair on top of his head, his pure baby-faced happiness. He was smiling in the picture and I try to remember the look of his real smiling, happy face. I'm also in the picture, at about three years old. I try to remember sitting there next to him. Sometimes I have success with memory and other times I don't. But I always think about Louis.

That's right. His name was Louis. My brother, Louis.

Sometimes I read the letter out loud to myself, try

to mimic the sound of my daddy's voice, to give it life again. Sometimes I don't.

"Dear Andre, if you get this it means your daddy is gone."

It finally seems true. I don't like remembering it, but I have to. Next, I skip down to my favorite part.

"First, I love you. That's important."

With that out of the way, Daddy gives me some advice.

"I always knew you would be a big, great man one day, but you didn't need to know it, at least not while I was around. At least, you didn't need to know it *too well*. The last thing on earth I wanted for you was to have a big head, or to grow up putting on airs, or to become full of yourself like I've seen happen to some other children. But not everyone always agreed with me on that."

I think about marsala lipstick. It's a color I can't hardly stand to see anymore. I told Uncle Melph that and he said he felt the same way. I keep on reading.

"That's what the second part of this letter is about, your real mama. Because if I'm gone, I don't know what kind of stories you might be hearing about our family's past. So, I want to make sure you get the straight dope from me, come hell or high water, once you're old enough to understand it."

Which I guess I finally am. Whether I am or not

doesn't matter, though, because I have to be. I'm the only one left to remember. I lay back on the big fluffy couch in my dressing room in New York City, open a Coke and read it again.

"Her name is Nola Hazmuka, and her family were big-timers back in the small town we grew up in. Dad was chief of police, uncle was a judge, and another uncle was the mayor. To top it off, her grandfather owned a bunch of real estate. I knew her since we were both little kids in Greensburg. We got married when she was just nineteen years old. Later we had you. And when you were two years old, we had Louis."

I look at the picture, look at his happy face. It always makes me smile, even when I'm sad.

"That's right. You had a baby brother. You remember, even if we never talk about it. I know you do. His name was Louis and I named him after my (and now your) favorite jazz musician. He was cute as a button. He would have been smart too, just like you. Here is a picture of him sitting next to you when you were just three years old. Just right before..."

I remember now. It's hard to believe it left my mind for so long. Or maybe it never really did, maybe I hid it behind other things. Maybe I had to do that. I keep reading.

"Well, there is no easy way to explain all this. I've never been a writer, but I will do my best. This is some stuff I had always planned on taking to my grave, and if you're reading this, I probably did. I hope at least knowing about it gives you some peace, Andre. I think you already know it but..."

This is the part where I always feel a lump in my throat, right near my scar, but I never stop reading, no matter what. I'm a soldier in the cause of happiness.

"Your mama was never very well. She was broken somehow. I can't explain it to you, but that was one of the reasons I was so in love with her. I always felt like she needed me. Like if I could just show her the right thing...well, here's where my writing fails me again. Suffice to say, she couldn't see a sunny day and smile. But sometimes I could point one out to her, and then it would be like all the clouds on earth parted just for one second. One thing she did have was big dreams. Expectations and things she wanted out of life which she reckoned would finally make her feel happy, but which no one could give her. She always expected so much. She was never really happy, that's just who she was. She had trouble with people. During our marriage, she had a big blow-up with her family and became estranged from her daddy and uncles. That's just a fancy way of saying they didn't speak to each other for a few years. It ended up that her father died, with them never making up, and when he died, Nola was not included in the will. She was cut out of the inheritance money, totally. Her old man donated all the money to colleges instead. Can you believe that? Well, I could. But Nola sure couldn't. When your mama found out about her father's death, she went into a deep depression. I mean deeper than deep."

I pause, like always, and wonder just how much of her is in me. I can feel it sometimes, her darkness. For a long time, I never recognized what it was, but now I know. It is there, on the edge of things, watching and waiting. I have to guard my happiness like a soldier in a watchtower.

"And in the worst part of her depression, that was when we had you. It was her idea. And I thought that having you, and Louis not long after, would make her happy again, give her purpose. But it didn't work. 'Cause the real secret is that some people just have a hole in them. They try to fill it their whole lives but sometimes they just never manage to. I fill mine with hard work, and with...well...with you. You can fill yours with music or art or another person. But Nola was one of those people who could never get that hole to stop eating her. She got worse. There were weeks at a time when I couldn't get her out of bed. She talked about killing herself. She hated everything about life in our small town, the pettiness of it. She felt trapped. She wanted something different, she said. But she could never say just what. Different is all. But I don't think I ever really understood what drove her to do what she ended up doing."

I remember it now. I remembered it always. The feel of the warm water, of safety and comfort and then—

Oh when the saints,
Go marching in...

"One night, Andre, while I was at work..."

The horror of it. The bathwater turning all red. The swirl of it around the drain. All of the red going round and round and finally disappearing away at the vanishing point. My head is getting light and—

Oh when the sun,
Refused to shine...

Mama had a beautiful singing voice. So deep and strong and lovely. She sang to Louis and me. I was getting sleepy. I was getting cold. And then—

Oh when the moon,
Turns red with blood...

"I worked for the railroad at the time, which kept me out overnight sometimes. She drank a bottle and went and got in the bathtub. She brought you two boys with her and..."

When I read this part, it makes me feel like I'm forcing Daddy to live it all over again. Even though he's dead. I know that. Every time I read him tell it, it feels like I'm doing him wrong. Anyway, I don't need him to tell it. All I needed was to just let myself remember.

I remember looking up at the bright overhead light on the bathroom ceiling, going all fuzzy. I remember her singing getting weaker.

Oh when the trumpet
Sounds its call

I keep reading the letter, no matter how hard it may be.

"Afterwards I thought...maybe your vocal works had been damaged. Because you didn't talk for so long. But it wasn't damage to your voice, was it? We never talked about it. I didn't know how to, and you got so quiet. So quiet you were afterwards, for years and years, which made me think maybe you had buried the horrible thing, that you kept Louis alive deep in your heart and that talking about it would only make it worse."

The razor in Mama's hand. The marsala paint chips on her fingernails. She hung her hand over the lip of the bathtub and let the little piece of metal drop onto the tile. Things were red. The vanishing point in the drain, with the swirls of our lives going round and round. I remember.

"She did herself first. But maybe her heart wasn't fully in it. I don't know why, but she didn't make deep enough cuts. That's why she lived, and why you lived.

But Louis. He was only one year old at the time and... Louis is gone now."

A tear rolls down my cheek, just like it does every time.

"With her late daddy having been chief of police, and her uncle a judge, she was able to get the whole business covered up somehow. But I took you and I left, as soon as I could. Then I made up a story about her running off from a truck stop. I told it so many times I started to believe it myself. Maybe you did too."

That's okay, Daddy. You did the right thing. You did the—

There's a knock at the door of my dressing room, and it pops me right out of these memories. I quickly put the letter away in its special place, set my Coke on the table and go to open it.

There, on the other side, are my three best friends in the world. That's right. I have friends now. They are standing there and waiting for me, all with smiling faces full of joy and happiness, smiles that I gave them.

I work in the cause of happiness. I smile back, put the dark memories away again for another day, for next time.

"Good show, my boy," says Mr. de Valencia.

"Great job, kid," Mr. Melancon says.

Felix high-fives me and says, "Alright, man, you really knocked them dead."

"Thanks."

"So, you must be exhausted, Andre. Are you ready to go back to New Orleans now?" Mr. de Valencia asks.

"There's just one stop I want to make first," I reply.

WHEN LOUIS ARMSTRONG DIED, he had already lived for seven decades. What a lucky man he turned out to be, the little waif from back of town, living in this grand city. His face, the one that used to hang low with dirty coins from the street corner, was on stamps and the cover of *Life*. His eyes, that used to stare out from the waif's home and cry, had seen the world a dozen times. His gravelly voice that used to talk to a coal mule was sent out into space.

But mainly, he got to have his time. In that way, he was luckier than my little brother by a whole lot. He was also luckier than my daddy, by about double. He also got to die in his bed, asleep and next to his wife, in a world that he thought was wonderful and that thought the same about him.

I come to the little gate in Flushing, which is a little further out from New York. I can see trees and grass again, and that makes me glad. I was beginning to think that New York didn't have any of those things, and I could see why he would have chosen this place.

Mr. de Valencia nods at me. "We will wait here for

you, Andre. Take your time." Mr. Melancon has his hat in his hands and Felix is sitting on a park bench doing the crossword puzzle of the Sunday *Times*, or trying anyway. He keeps asking us for the answers. But of course, we don't know.

I walk down a little pathway alone, getting deeper into the place. It is full summer now, but it isn't so hot as home gets this time of year. The air is drier and thinner, and it feels like fall could be right around the corner.

I still think about his voice flying out into space, forever and ever. The sound of his trumpet never finds the vanishing point. It lives on and just keeps on going. But not his body. It has a vanishing point, just like all bodies do, and that is right here in Flushing.

"Hi, Louis," I say.

The stone is plain black, and the word "Satchmo" is etched into the thing. Next to him is Lucille, his final and longest wife. He is lying there under my feet. The real man. Not just some statue or picture or video.

On top of his tombstone there is a little horn made of stone, and people have left all sorts of gifts. There are Mardi Gras beads of all colors and shapes, draped over half the thing. There are coins stacked in little piles here and there, and I'm surprised that no one has taken them. People have also stacked stones and someone has even left a little wooden carving of a trumpet.

"You aren't my brother," I say. "Of course, I know that."

I feel awkward for a second and squat down to be closer to him, my voice falling to a whisper. There are a few other folks in the graveyard and I want to be sure they don't hear.

"And I know...you aren't my daddy, either. In fact, we never met or knew each other at all. But I've read and thought about you so much, I guess I do kind of know you, in a way. It took me a long time, Louis, to realize what I was doing. I just couldn't think about some things. Some things were just too awful. And when I couldn't think about those things, when I couldn't or wouldn't remember...I'd think about you instead."

He doesn't answer, of course. He's been dead for fifty years.

"You never will know who I am or what I will be one day, but I still wanted to thank you for everything you've ever done for me. I loved my dead brother Louis and my dead daddy, but I also love you."

I heard a rustle in the branches just over my head. There's a bluebird there, cocking his head at me and looking down. He tweets a little song at me before flying away.

"Now that I've told you that, Louis, I'll be going back to New Orleans."

He still doesn't say anything, but I know a smile when I feel it.

I take a silver-dollar coin out of my pocket and I put it on top of the stone.

Then I go home.

THE END

AFTERWORD

Only **you** can solve Herbert and Melancon's next big mystery.

You've finished "Uptown Blues," and I hope you've enjoyed it. I put a lot of hours into making it the best reader experience possible, and I hope that came across in the words. As a small-time indie writer, those hours spent have to be budgeted out of a real life in which I spend forty plus hours a week running three businesses.

The point is (you probably guessed it), this is the part where I ask you for a **review**!

You see, as an indie writer, I am made or broken by exposure. If I get exposure, in the form of reviews, word of mouth, Goodreads lists, Twitter posts - or whatever else has lots of avid readers looking and talking - it means I'm able to succeed.

That publishing success, in turn, means I'm able to

whittle away a few more hours from my business demands in order to write more words for you. Which means book number six will be here all the sooner. Which is what I desperately want.

I hope that is what you want, too.

So please, let the world know if you enjoy my work. The more you do that, the faster Felix and Melancon can get to the bottom of their next crazy, deadly, intriguing, New Orleans-y adventure!

They are both counting on you, dear reader. And so am I!

Please leave a review – Amazon, Goodreads, Facebook, Reddit, Twitter – whatever! You can also sign up for my mailing list at my blog: https://sethpevey.com/, for future updates, giveaways, and possibly even advanced beta-reader status!

Help Herbert and Melancon keep letting the good times roll, and I'll see you in **book number six**!

Printed in Great Britain
by Amazon

77031636R00180